JOURNEY
TO THE
LIGHTS

Copyright © 2016 Disney Enterprises, Inc. All rights reserved. Published in the United States by Random House Children's Books, a division of Penguin Random House LLC, 1745 Broadway, New York, NY 10019, and in Canada by Penguin Random House Canada Limited, Toronto, in conjunction with Disney Enterprises, Inc. Random House and the colophon are registered trademarks of Penguin Random House LLC.
Photos provided by Superstock.
randomhousekids.com
ISBN 978-0-7364-3659-5 (hardcover)
Printed in the United States of America
10 9 8 7 6 5 4 3 2 1
Random House Children's Books supports the First Amendment and celebrates the right to read.

JOURNEY
TO THE
LIGHTS

by Suzanne Francis

Random House 🏠 New York

CHAPTER
1

QUEEN ELSA AND PRINCESS ANNA raced around their bedrooms anxiously getting ready . . . and trying their best not to look at the time. Their good friend Kristoff had invited them on an adventure, but he had kept the details a secret. Whenever they asked questions about where they were going, he would cheerfully say, "A true adventure is full of surprises, and this is going to be a true adventure."

All day long, the sisters had busied themselves with little tasks around the castle, trying to keep their eyes off that seemingly lazy clock. They'd been told to meet Kristoff in the courtyard at three, and now that it was finally after two, they felt as if they might burst.

Anna knocked on Elsa's bedroom door. "Two-fifteen!" she called.

Elsa popped out of her room and grinned. "I know," she said.

They ran downstairs to the foyer, nearly bumping into Gerda and Kai, longtime castle servants and family friends. "Oops, sorry!"

said Anna. "We're just a little excited."

Gerda and Kai smiled at the sisters. They hadn't seen them behave this way in quite some time. "Yes, we can see that," said Gerda. "Why don't you sit down and relax for a bit?"

Kai agreed. "You do still have a little time before you have to meet Kristoff. Would you like some tea?"

There was no way they could have a cup of tea—they were way too excited! "No thanks," said Elsa. "But sitting down for a few minutes does sound like a good idea."

The sisters sat beside each other in the foyer and immediately began talking about the few things Kristoff *had* told them.

"He said we didn't have to bring anything,"

Anna said slowly, as if trying to decode his words. "Do you think we're going to harvest ice?"

"I don't think so," said Elsa. "Since we've harvested ice with him before, I don't think he'd see that as a surprise."

"It will be dark soon," said Anna, gazing out the window at the autumn sky. "Maybe it's a campfire . . . with music. A sing-along?"

"Or . . . maybe we're going to look at the stars?" offered Elsa.

They continued to try to figure out where they could be going, but Kristoff hadn't offered many clues. They recalled what he had told them earlier: "It's something you've never seen before," he'd said. "You've probably never even heard of it!"

"How can we possibly guess if we don't even know it exists?" asked Elsa.

"I can't stand the wait any longer!" Anna eyed the clock. "Fifteen minutes," she cheered, rapidly tapping her feet on the floor.

Elsa grinned. "It will take us at least two to get to the courtyard."

The sisters sprang from their chairs, said goodbye to Gerda and Kai, and rushed out of the castle and into the courtyard.

Kristoff and his reindeer, Sven, were ready and waiting. They had arrived early, too, and seemed just as impatient as the girls.

As they greeted each other, their friend Olaf ran toward them, waving his twig hand.

"I'm ready for the super-secret adventure!" he announced. Ever since Elsa had built him, the cheerful snowman had become a part of their family. No journey would be complete without him.

"Great," said Kristoff. "We're all here, so let's go." He began leading the way.

"So . . . ?" Anna said eagerly, walking alongside him. "Can you tell us where we're going now?"

Kristoff smiled, thoroughly enjoying keeping the secret. "Well," he said, pausing. "We're going up into the mountains."

"Up into the mountains," Anna repeated. "Okay. And . . . what are we doing once we get up into the mountains?" She tried digging for more information, to no avail.

"Oh, I can't tell you that," Kristoff teased. "It would ruin the surprise. And a true adventure—"

"Is full of surprises," said Elsa and Anna together, finishing Kristoff's sentence for him.

"We know, we know!" said Anna.

The sisters groaned in frustration. They had to find out where they were going!

Kristoff laughed. "Okay, okay," he said. "I won't torture you any longer. . . . We're going to Troll Valley for the annual crystal ceremony!"

Elsa and Anna's eyes widened with excitement, and their pace quickened as they started up the path. They were intrigued by what little they knew about trolls and their mysterious ways. They had both visited the trolls on several occasions and knew that the elder troll, Grand Pabbie, was a wise and kind leader. They also knew that trolls used crystals. But Kristoff was right—they had never heard of the crystal ceremony before.

"Every year, Grand Pabbie honors the young trolls who have earned all their level-one crystals," Kristoff explained. "It's a huge achievement. And the ceremony is incredible." He had wonderful memories of ceremonies he had attended over the years and was certain his friends would love the experience as much as he did.

Anna's and Elsa's minds filled with

questions as Kristoff went on to tell them the ceremony happened once a year, during autumn, and could only be performed under the bright Northern Lights. "The lights never look as amazing as they do during the crystal ceremony," he added.

The girls gasped at the mention of the Northern Lights, which had fascinated them since they were young. The thought of the lights reminded them of their childhood adventures. It wasn't just the beauty of the lights they loved; it was the mystery as well. Why were the lights sometimes green and sometimes pink? Why did the colors sometimes swirl together? One thing Anna and Elsa knew for sure: they loved watching the lights—especially when they were colorful and bright.

"Oh, I love the Northern Lights," agreed Olaf. "They're like a giant sky party."

Kristoff told them that this year's ceremony was going to be very special—and not just because his friends were joining him for the first time. There was another reason. When they asked him to explain, he smiled that sly smile again and said, "You'll see." He didn't want to hand over all his secrets just yet!

As they came up to a clearing near a cluster of pine trees, Kristoff paused.

"Are we here already?" Olaf asked, looking around. Whenever Olaf visited Troll Valley, the trolls would unroll from their rock form to greet him. He glanced down at a nearby boulder. "Hello, troll friend," he said, patting the boulder. "It's so nice to see you again. You look well." When the rock didn't reveal itself as a friendly troll, Olaf turned to Kristoff and whispered, "Why isn't he saying hello? Is he still sleeping?"

Kristoff shook his head. "No, we're not there yet. That's an ordinary rock."

"Well, it was a nice rock anyway," Olaf said, turning away from the rock and seeing Sven, who was standing awfully close to Olaf's face.

"Hi, Sven," Olaf said. Drool dripped from Sven's lips as he leaned in even closer. "How are you today?"

Kristoff looked at Olaf with a grin. "I think he wants a snack," he said.

Anna and Elsa giggled.

"Ohhhhh, I get it," said Olaf. "I've told you before, Sven. Eating noses is not very polite. Remember?" He softly patted Sven's nose and cooed, "Who's a good reindeer? Who's a good reindeer?"

"Let's stop at Oaken's," said Kristoff. "We can pick up carrots there." Sven trotted ahead, leading the way through the pine forest to the trading post.

The bell on top of the door jingled as the group walked into Wandering Oaken's Trading Post and Sauna.

"Hoo-hoo," sang Oaken, the giant,

friendly owner of the trading post. "Anyone like a sauna? Double punch on your frequent sauna card today." He held up a little card.

"A sauna sounds lovely!" exclaimed Olaf.

"Uh, we don't have time for that today," said Elsa, quickly guiding Olaf away from the sauna. "Let's look around."

"Ooh, look! Jars of things," said Olaf, distracted by a shelf full of trinkets.

Anna scanned the store for a notebook. Since hearing about the crystal ceremony, she thought it would be great to include in the history of Arendelle. She figured they could write about the details of the event and keep a record of it in the castle library. Seeing nothing on the shelves, she approached the counter and asked Oaken if he had any journals for sale.

Oaken eyed an empty shelf. "Too bad," he said. "Just finished up a big notebook blowout." He shuffled through some drawers behind the counter. "But . . . I do have this one." He blew the dust off an old used journal. The leather cover was worn, and several pages were crumpled and creased. "It has some writing in it, but most of the pages are blank. Thirty percent off. *Ja?*"

"I'll take it," said Anna, wiping off the cover and tucking the book under her arm.

Kristoff grabbed a bunch of carrots and placed them on the counter.

"Hoo-hoo, Kristoff," said Oaken. "Before

you go, I must show you." He walked toward the wall and picked up a bundle of rope hanging on a nail, then held it toward Kristoff. "It's part of our new winter stock."

"We don't need any rope, but thanks," said Kristoff.

"Not just any rope," Oaken explained. "This is brand-new, super-strong rope of my own invention. It can hold and pull almost anything. Your life is actually quite incomplete without it. *Ja?*"

"It's a convincing argument," Kristoff mumbled to Anna.

"We'll take that, too." Anna smiled. "Thank you." She turned to Kristoff and whispered, "It might come in handy."

They paid for their goods and headed for the exit. "Bye-bye," Oaken sang. "Come again soon."

As they left the trading post, Sven, who had been anxiously waiting outside, bounced over and began sniffing Kristoff, searching for the carrots.

"Here you go, buddy," Kristoff said, handing him one. Sven happily chomped down on the tasty carrot.

The friends continued their hike, enjoying one another's company. The towering pine trees made the air smell fresh, and the autumn wind felt cool against their cheeks. Anna and Elsa asked Kristoff questions about the crystal ceremony, and Anna jotted notes in the journal along the way. It wasn't long before they had reached the top of the mountain.

When they started down the other side, the terrain changed dramatically. The land became rocky, with patches of moss scattered about. Steam rose slowly from vents in the ground. Instead of lush pine trees, the area was dotted with young birch saplings that had shed the bulk of their leaves. As the sun started making its way behind the mountain range, they reached the jagged cliffs overlooking Troll Valley.

When they stepped down onto the rocky ground of the valley, there was a sudden shift in the air. Everything was strangely quiet and still. Even the few leaves that dangled from the trees appeared to stop shaking. Instinctively, everyone halted and looked around, waiting for something to happen.

Then a booming, cheerful voice cut through the silence. "They're here!"

In a flash, dozens of large, round, mossy rocks rolled across the ground from every corner of the valley and circled them.

CHAPTER 2

THE ROCKS STOPPED AND POPPED open, revealing that they weren't rocks at all, but trolls! Short, thick, and chunky, they had large, pointed ears and big, bulging noses. Grassy mounds of hair sprouted from the top of their heads above close-set, joyful eyes. Their clothing was made of moss, and some of them wore necklaces decorated with glowing crystals. With their hard, round bodies and big hands and feet, they truly looked like living rocks.

The friendly little trolls were thrilled to see Kristoff and his friends. They hopped onto one another's shoulders to be face to face with their guests. With lots of cheers and chatter, they greeted the group warmly.

Bulda gave Kristoff an extra-tight squeeze. "I'm so happy you're here," she said.

"Me too," said Kristoff. He had met Bulda when he was a young child. He never knew his own parents, but Bulda had taken Sven and him in when they'd had no one else. She had treated them like part of the family and, though she could be a little pushy sometimes,

Kristoff loved her very much and was always glad to see her.

"It's nice to see you here too, Anna," Bulda said with a knowing smile. She adored Anna and was always happy to see her spending time with Kristoff. If she could have arranged their marriage, she would have—in fact, she had tried to the very first time she had met Anna!

Suddenly, a young troll came barreling through the crowd. "Kristoff!" he shouted as he nearly tackled Kristoff to the ground with a giant hug. The troll was small compared to Kristoff, but much heavier than he looked.

"Whoa," said Kristoff, regaining his balance. "Hi, Little Rock!"

The eager little troll tried to help steady Kristoff and nearly knocked him over again. "Sorry," he said. "I'm just so excited! I can't believe it's finally time!"

Kristoff's smile widened. He proudly introduced the troll to his friends and revealed his second surprise: this year's ceremony was extra special because Little Rock, who was like family to Kristoff, was going to be in it. They had shared lots of great times, and after seeing all of Little Rock's hard work, Kristoff was proud to celebrate him and his accomplishments.

"That's wonderful! I'm so happy to meet you," said Anna.

Everyone congratulated Little Rock and

told him how excited they were to be there. Little Rock beamed. He couldn't wait to share this special occasion with the whole group.

"So when does the ceremony begin?" asked Elsa.

"Well, let's see . . . three days left of autumn, so . . ." Kristoff pretended to calculate in his head. "It better start soon." He looked over at Bulda. "Right?"

"Oh, yes," she replied. "The ceremony must take place in autumn under the bright Northern Lights."

"Why is that?" asked Anna, eager to know all the details.

Bulda climbed on top of a boulder so she

could be seen and heard around the valley. She proclaimed:

"We Guardians of Earth do know
Autumn lights and crystals glow
So our bond may deepen and grow."

Anna whispered to Elsa, "Did you understand that?"

Elsa shrugged. "Troll wisdom can be very confusing."

The girls smiled and nodded politely at Bulda, figuring they would just go with it.

Anna approached Little Rock and knelt beside him. "I'd love to see your crystals."

"Sure!" said Little Rock, happy to share. "I keep them in here so they stay safe and sound." He proudly pulled a small, dark pouch out of his pocket, then leaned in and whispered, "We're not allowed to wear the cyrstals around our necks until we get to level three."

Anna smiled and nodded, feeling like she had just learned a troll secret.

Little Rock loosened the string around the pouch and a blue glow seeped out, reflecting light in his hand. He pulled out one of the small glowing crystals and showed it to Anna. "This is my water crystal," he explained.

"Wow," Anna said, admiring it. The glow of the crystal seemed to make the air around it buzz. "It's amazing."

Little Rock pulled another crystal from the

pouch. "This is my snow crystal." He held it out to Anna and she gratefully placed the crystal in her hand. It felt cool and smooth, like a piece of glass. It was really beautiful, too, but it looked just like the other one.

Little Rock held up a third crystal. "And this is my ice crystal."

The ice crystal looked identical to the other two. Little Rock continued to describe the other glowing crystals in his pouch: there was a harvesting crystal, a camouflaging crystal, an honesty crystal, and a stargazing crystal. Every one of them had a similar blue glow.

"How can you tell the difference?" Anna asked.

"I don't know exactly how to explain that,"

Little Rock said with a chuckle. "It's a troll thing." He shrugged. "They all look the same to Kristoff, too."

"Well, they're really beautiful," said Anna. Then she noticed a dull crystal peeking from the corner of the open pouch. "What about that one?" she asked, pointing it out.

"My tracking crystal," Little Rock said with a sigh. "It won't glow until I have excellent tracking skills. It's my last level-one crystal."

"Oh," said Anna. "Does that mean you need to earn it before . . . ?"

"That's right," he said sadly. "If I don't earn it in time, I can't be in the ceremony."

Anna was surprised. If the ceremony *had* to happen in the next few days, did Little

Rock have the time to earn it? Anna decided she would try to help Little Rock any way she could.

"I don't really understand why it's not glowing," said Little Rock. "I've been tracking all kinds of things: worms, bugs, my uncle Emil." An old, tired troll shuffled by and waved.

Little Rock pointed to a bird pecking at tiny red berries on the ground nearby. "I even tracked him through the valley all day long." He held up the dull crystal and inspected it. Then he gave it a shake and flicked it a few times with his finger. "But nothing—not even a tiny spark."

Kristoff gently placed a hand on Little Rock's shoulder. "But it takes more than just following, Little Rock. Remember the three rules of tracking?" Kristoff held up a finger for each rule as he recited it. "Be fearless, be observant, be inventive."

"I remember," said Little Rock. "And I try to be all those things." He lowered his head. "But I don't know if I can."

"Of course you can," said Kristoff, giving him a playful shove. "You just need to venture out of the valley and really track something— put those rules to work. Then you'll find your confidence." He smiled at Little Rock. "*And* earn your tracking crystal."

Little Rock looked down at his feet. "I guess I'm a little nervous. I haven't really gone outside the valley," he murmured. "What if I get lost and can't find my way back home?"

"You can do it, Little Rock," said Kristoff. "I know you can."

Anna and Elsa gave him some encouraging words as well, but Little Rock barely heard them. Darkness covered the valley. When Little Rock looked up at the sky, he gasped.

"Look at those clouds!" he said, pointing. Night had fallen, and a thick layer of cloud cover had rolled in like a creeping fog, obscuring the moonlight.

"They don't look very friendly," Olaf said as the dark clouds spread across the sky.

"This can't be good," said Little Rock, his face filled with worry. "If we can't see the Northern Lights, there won't even *be* a ceremony!"

CHAPTER 3

"IT'S OKAY, LITTLE ROCK," SAID ONE of the older trolls, smiling to reveal several missing teeth. "It will pass."

"But if—" Little Rock was cut off by another troll wearing many glowing crystals around her neck.

"You worry too much," she said, waving her hand dismissively. "Many autumn nights are cloudy. And many aren't. It will be fine."

Little Rock looked at her incredulously. "But if we can't see the Northern Lights, Grand Pabbie can't perform the ceremony, and autumn is almost over and—" Little Rock's voice trembled. "What will we do if there's no crystal ceremony this year?"

Elsa and Anna didn't know what to say. They were wondering the same thing.

Rather than providing answers, the other trolls offered soothing words, attempting to calm Little Rock's worries. But Little Rock simply couldn't calm down, and his worry grew and grew.

"Where is Grand Pabbie?" he asked, looking through the crowd. He knew he had to find him to get answers. "Grand Pabbie! Where are you?"

He hopped up onto a rocky ledge and looked out across the valley, continuing to search and call out for the elder troll, but he was nowhere to be found.

"All right," said Kristoff. "We'll figure this out."

"What if we don't?" asked Little Rock, hopping down off the ledge. "Why would Grand Pabbie leave now?"

Bulda stepped toward Little Rock, shaking her head.

"Stop, Little Rock," she said. "Don't worry. Grand Pabbie probably just went to find a new site where the Northern Lights *are* visible. This has happened before. I'm sure it will all work out fine."

Little Rock took a few deep breaths and tried to calm down. Bulda assured him the ceremony would still go on.

"But what if I'm not there?" he asked quietly. "I'll get left behind and everyone else will move ahead."

Bulda comforted him. "Where you will be is up to you," she said.

Little Rock tried to stop a frown from creeping across his face, but he felt frustrated. He didn't have time to try to decode Bulda's words. There was no way he would miss the crystal ceremony. He needed to do something, and *fast* . . . but he didn't know what.

Kristoff could see how upset Little Rock was and tried to think of a way to help. Then he had an idea.

"Why don't we track Grand Pabbie?" he suggested. "We can find Grand Pabbie *and* you can earn your crystal."

Little Rock's body quaked with excitement, and his worried expression turned into a giant grin. "A *real* tracking quest? With all of you?" he said, smiling up at Kristoff and his friends.

"We would love to help you, Little Rock," said Anna.

"Of course we would," agreed Elsa.

"I love quests!" said Olaf. "What's a quest?"

"A quest is a kind of adventure where you're searching for something—in this case, it's Grand Pabbie," Kristoff explained.

"What an amazing idea!" exclaimed Little Rock, jumping up and down. He started running around in circles, unsure how to get himself ready for the big trip. "I'll get my tracking crystal *and* I'll get to hang out with Kristoff and my new friends. I'm the luckiest troll in Troll Valley!"

Bulda thought it was an excellent idea and smiled proudly at Kristoff and his friends. "Wonderful!" she said. "Helping a young troll is an honorable duty."

Once he stopped running in circles, Little Rock grabbed Kristoff's and Anna's hands and tried to lead them out of the valley.

"All right! Let's go! I'm *so* ready to start this

quest!" he cheered as he pulled Kristoff and Anna.

"It could be a long trip," Bulda warned. "I think all of you should rest here tonight and set out tomorrow."

Little Rock deflated slightly. He didn't want to wait an entire day to start their journey. Kristoff noticed his disappointment. "Don't worry, Little Rock. We have three whole days—there's still plenty of time to find Grand Pabbie. We'll set out first thing tomorrow night."

"Yes, it'll be great," Anna said. "We'll be all rested and ready to go!"

Little Rock brightened again. "You're right. I can wait until tomorrow. Crystal ceremony, here we come!"

Everyone cheered. They couldn't wait to start their adventure!

The next night, the group prepared to leave Troll Valley. Little Rock was thrilled at the prospect of earning his tracking crystal with his friends.

"Our quest begins today!" he exclaimed. "Pretty soon, we'll find Grand Pabbie, I'll have my tracking crystal, and we can start the ceremony!"

Kristoff, Anna, and Elsa couldn't help smiling at Little Rock's enthusiasm. His eagerness was infectious!

Just before they left, Bulda stopped them. "You better take some warmer cloaks so you don't get cold," she said.

Before they could even respond, a group of trolls appeared, carrying special cloaks made of moss and leaves.

Elsa politely declined. "That's very kind of you," she said. "But the cold never bothers me."

"I would love one!" Olaf said happily.

Anna and Kristoff accepted the cloaks as well, and let the trolls put them on.

"I feel like a forest," said Olaf, twirling around to make the cloak flare out like a cape. He twirled faster and faster . . . until the cloak flew right off and landed in a tree! "It's so light and airy," he said, still twirling and completely unaware that he was no longer wearing the cloak.

Kristoff looked at Anna wearing the mossy thing around her shoulders and couldn't help thinking of the first time he had brought her to Troll Valley. The trolls had dressed both of them in ceremonial crowns and cloaks made of moss, twigs, and leaves. Then they had attempted to marry them! Kristoff recalled feeling completely ridiculous as he stood there staring at Anna. They smiled at each other now, and Kristoff knew they were both thinking back to that day.

"You better get going," Bulda said. She looked up at the sky, then turned to them and declared:

"AS THE SUN RESTS ITS SLEEPY HEAD,
WE TROLLS MUST WAKE FROM SLUMBERING
BED; OUR DUTIES TO THE EARTH BE MADE
BEFORE THE STARS AND MOON DO FADE."

Elsa and Anna exchanged a look and shrugged. Anna leaned over to Kristoff. "Translation, please?" she whispered.

"Trolls sleep during the day and do stuff at night," he explained.

"Right," Anna said, nodding. "I knew that."

"I'm ready," said Little Rock, checking to make sure his crystal pouch was securely fastened. He smiled.

With the autumn clock ticking fast, they didn't have much time to find Grand Pabbie before the ceremony. They prepared to leave and said goodbye to the trolls.

Bulda gave Kristoff another tight squeeze. "See you soon—and good luck," she said.

The trolls wished Little Rock lots of luck on his quest and waved.

"Thank you, everybody!" called Little Rock as he left with Kristoff and his new friends.

The stars twinkled above as the group started back up the rocky cliffs, climbing from ledge to ledge. They felt energized. Elsa and Anna couldn't believe the unexpected turn in their adventure. Who ever would have thought thcy would bc going on a nighttime tracking quest with a little troll?

"Well, you were right, Kristoff," said Anna.

"About what?"

"A true adventure is—"

"Full of surprises," Kristoff finished. "So it's official. This is a true adventure for everyone. Even me."

CHAPTER 4

ONCE LITTLE ROCK AND HIS FRIENDS
made it to the top of the cliffs overlooking
Troll Valley, they had a great view of the
massive mountain ranges in the distance. Elsa
pointed out faint wisps of green Northern
Lights dancing in the sky above one of the
mountaintops. Even though the lights were
dim, the sight gave everyone a jolt of awe.

They watched the lights for a few moments.

"See, Little Rock, the Northern Lights haven't disappeared," Elsa said. "Maybe we should head that way?"

"That's exactly what I was thinking!" said Little Rock. He jumped ahead of the group, taking the lead as everyone followed him. The path wound up the mountain, and the terrain became less and less rocky.

As they hiked, Little Rock prattled on about random tracking facts. "Trolls have been tracking since ancient times. The ancients used to say it was like reading the earth." He laughed. "But they used to say it in a much fancier-sounding way, of course." Little Rock made his voice sound deep and mystical as he pretended to be a wise old troll. "'Of soil and scent, the trolls do know, they track to find . . .'" He coughed a few times and went back to speaking in his regular voice. "Something, something, something." Little Rock smiled up at them and laughed, a little embarrassed. "I can't remember the rest, but that's the basic idea."

"That's okay," said Anna. "We appreciate hearing the simple version of troll wisdom."

"Yes," Elsa agreed. "The ancient troll-speak can get a little confusing for us."

"I know what you mean," said Little Rock. He hopped up onto a tree stump along the path and didn't see its rotted-out center. One of his feet fell right into the hole and became wedged inside. "Anyway, trolls are natural trackers." He tried to act natural while attempting to free his foot. "And for level-one trolls like me, it's really just a matter of tapping into it." Little Rock struggled, unable to get his chunky foot out of the hole.

"That is very true," said Kristoff, bending down and shifting Little Rock's foot just the right way to get it out of the stump.

"Thanks, Kristoff," Little Rock said. He smiled and jumped back onto the path, running ahead of everyone to take the lead.

"Trolls are naturally excellent trackers," said Kristoff.

"We really are," said Little Rock.

Suddenly, Little Rock came to an abrupt

stop, causing everyone to halt behind him. The mountain path split in three different directions. He wasn't sure which to choose. He paused as he examined the options. His eyes flickered from one to the other and then back again as he nervously wiggled his fingers and toes, deep in contemplation.

Finally, he glanced over at Kristoff, hoping for a clue. It was obvious to Kristoff: Little Rock was afraid he was about to choose the wrong path.

"That goes *back* to Troll Valley," said Kristoff, gesturing to the first path.

Little Rock stared intently at the remaining two paths, his fingers and toes still wiggling away. He glanced at Kristoff again, then slowly raised his foot and took a baby step toward the middle path.

"That's toward Arendelle," whispered Anna. Little Rock quickly took a baby step back again. Everyone knew that trolls usually avoided places with lots of humans.

With only one choice left, Little Rock nodded and started down the third path. "This way!" he shouted in his most confident voice.

The group continued walking up the mountain, and Little Rock babbled on, telling them all about different tracking theories and stories. One of them involved twin trolls who could track each other from opposite sides of the globe. Another was about an ancient troll with only one nostril who could sniff out scents from as far as twenty miles away. He talked about tracking patterns in soil, sand, mud, and even water. Everyone enjoyed listening to Little Rock ramble, but they had to wonder how much of what he said was actually true!

Suddenly, Little Rock held up his hand and shouted, "Hold on, everyone!" The group stopped in their tracks and looked at him, waiting to see what he would do next. "I'm picking up a scent," he said, his nose twitching as he lifted his head and smelled the air.

"Trolls have an incredible sense of smell," Kristoff whispered to the others as they all stood around watching Little Rock work.

"I think it's Grand Pabbie," said Little Rock. He dropped to the ground and began sniffing every inch of it, following the scent this way and that, zigzagging about until he finally reached the source of the smell.

A hoof! Little Rock looked up to see a reindeer staring back at him.

"Um, that's Sven," Kristoff said gently.

Little Rock chuckled over his mistake. "Oops! I guess I got a little overeager. I just can't wait to use my tracking skills and find Grand Pabbie!"

"It's okay," said Anna. "We're all very excited—and nervous. So we completely understand how you feel."

"I think you're doing a wonderful job," said Olaf.

"And now we know you can track Sven if we lose him," Elsa added.

Little Rock couldn't help smiling. He was grateful to have such wonderful new friends.

"I have an idea," offered Elsa. "How about a story to take your mind off things and relax you a bit?"

"Ooh, I love stories," said Olaf.

"That's a great idea," said Anna.

Kristoff agreed. "The path keeps going up this way," he said. "So we should be okay to just follow it for a while without having to make any decisions. What do you think, Little Rock?"

"I think you're right." Little Rock licked his finger and held it up, as if testing the air. "Yes," he said, nodding while wearing a serious expression. "I think now would be the perfect time for a story. We follow the path while we listen to it. It's a perfect plan." Little Rock smiled at Elsa. "Did you have one you were going to tell?"

"I was thinking about sharing my favorite memory of the Northern Lights. And I bet Anna can help me." Elsa smiled at her sister. "What do the lights make *you* think of, Anna?" she asked.

Anna's eyes sparkled with anticipation. She knew exactly what Elsa meant.

Anna began the story. . . .

CHAPTER 5

ᴀɴɴᴀ: When we were little girls, we loved the Northern Lights. But we could never seem to catch more than a glimpse. We'd spot them from a window of the castle high up in the sky or see them reflected in the fjord and we'd get so excited. But the sighting was always too brief. Not long after it became dark, we would get shuffled off to bed. We were never allowed to stay up late or go outside beyond the castle walls at night to really see them.

We used to ask our parents if they would let us stay up and look for the lights. We wanted to go far from the castle—we figured that going somewhere dark would be the best way to truly see the lights at their brightest and most colorful.

ELSA: I think we must have asked them a hundred times. And a hundred times they said no. They gave us plenty of reasons: "Children must go to sleep early." "You need your rest." "You can see the lights from your window." But none of those reasons made us stop thinking about seeing the lights.

ANNA: Then one night, instead of telling us a story and tucking us into bed, Mama and Papa had a surprise. They brought us outside and tucked us into the carriage instead!

Papa smiled and said, "I think tonight is a good night to go hunting for those Northern Lights.

What do you girls think?" You could hear the joy in his voice—he was so proud of himself for surprising us.

Gerda and Kai gave us cups of hot cocoa and we sat in the back of the carriage under a blanket. I remember Gerda whispering, "Have fun, Princesses." We just beamed and giggled. We were completely speechless!

ELSA: That didn't happen very often.

ANNA: We were both so shocked. I still remember the look on your face!

Anyway, we sat, snug and

cozy as the horses pulled the carriage past the castle gates and over the bridge. We watched Arendelle disappear into the distance as Papa drove all the way to the foot of the north mountain range—which looked completely different at night.

Mama and Papa helped us out of the carriage and we all started hiking up the mountain. We couldn't believe they were taking us on such an adventure. The night was black, but a million sparkling stars and a beautiful full moon gave us enough light to see where we were going.

When we got to the top of the mountain, there was a clearing with a beautiful meadow. Papa and Mama set out a blanket. They gazed up at the stars and asked us if we wanted to sit with them.

There was no way that was going to happen! We couldn't sit down when there was so much to see and do! We ran through the meadow and went off to explore. We played hide-and-seek in the dark, hiding in the tall grass, behind boulders and trees—

ELSA: Jumping out and scaring

each other—BOO!

ANNA: Ahh! Elsa!

ELSA: We were having a great time and had completely forgotten the whole point of the trip. It really didn't matter whether or not we saw the Northern Lights.

ANNA: But then, out of nowhere—with no warning—these amazingly bright pink and green ribbons of light appeared and rippled across the night sky. It was like nothing we had ever seen before. We both gasped and just stood there together, staring up and watching them in absolute awe.

I wanted to get closer, so I started running up the mountain. . . . Wait a second. I thought we were at the top of the mountain? Was there a hill or . . . ?

ELSA: No. There wasn't a hill.

ANNA: Did we climb a tree? No. That's not right. My memory is definitely hazy on this one.

ELSA: I used my powers to make a staircase out of snow.

ANNA: Okay, yeah. That makes a lot more sense. I do remember running up toward the lights, higher and higher. But of course, I don't remember the magical snow staircase part. Tell me all about it!

ELSA: I made this staircase that swirled up toward the lights. We chased each other as I continued to build it higher and higher. It was like we were running up into the sky. We should have been scared—in fact, I was a little nervous. But you refused to stop, so we kept going!

ANNA: Then what happened? We ran up to the very top, right?

ELSA: Well, sort of. We chased each other until we simply couldn't run anymore. We sat down at the top, completely out of breath.

ANNA: I remember. We sat right next to each other and watched the lights. They filled the entire sky. I can still see them in my mind. They were more gorgeous and mysterious than I ever could have imagined. And we wondered if they were like wishing stars. . . . Remember?

ELSA: I do.

ANNA: We thought the Northern Lights were even better than wishing stars. Maybe they were like the biggest, most powerful wishing star ever. And we decided we'd better make a wish just in case we were right. We closed our eyes and— Do you remember our wish?

ELSA: Of course. We wished for more adventures like that one together . . . even when we got big.

ANNA: That's right. Then, as if the lights heard our wish, the sky responded, and it started to snow! A gentle flurry made everything around us shimmer with the colors of the lights. Wait a second . . . was that you?

ELSA: It was me.

ANNA: Nice touch.

ANNA & ELSA: It was amazing.

CHAPTER 6

"Wow," said Little Rock. "What an incredible adventure!"

Elsa knew the power of stories and was hoping the tale might do more than just take Little Rock's mind off his worries for a moment; she hoped it would help him look at things a little differently. "See, Little Rock?" she said, nudging him along. "New experiences may be scary at first, but they can turn into true adventures."

"That's right," said Anna. She knew what Elsa was trying to do. Their parents had done the same thing to them when they were little. Like buried treasures, there were always hidden lessons and thoughts tucked somewhere inside the wonderful stories they would share. "If you let fear take over, you might miss out on something wonderful."

"I know what you mean," Little Rock agreed. "I used to be afraid to try thistle because I thought it would pinch my throat. But once I got over my fear and just popped it in my mouth, it was wonderfully delicious! And surprisingly smooth. It's actually my favorite snack now. But of course, only trolls should eat it." He held his head high and walked with a little extra spring in his step.

Kristoff smiled at Anna and Elsa. "He totally gets it," he said, trying to stifle a laugh.

"Look," said Little Rock, pointing to a nearby peak. "We're almost to the top of the mountain. Let's run!" The troll ran ahead and the group trotted behind him up the steep incline until the ground leveled out.

Once at the very top, they looked over the ridge to see the mountain range spread out before them. Where could Grand Pabbie be? There was still plenty of ground left to cover.

Little Rock pointed out a light dusting of snow and wiggled his toes through it.

"Snow!" Olaf cheered. "If I had toes, I'd be wiggling them, too."

"It is definitely colder up here," Anna said, pulling her mossy cloak around her.

The group continued to walk across the plateau until they came to a frozen river. Kristoff reminded everyone to walk carefully as they started to make their way across.

Little Rock tapped on the ice with his foot a few times. "Oh, don't worry," he said. "I know ice. I did earn my ice crystal, remember?" He chuckled. "And this ice is extremely thick. I can tell." Little Rock skipped ahead to the front of the group once again to be sure he remained the leader. "No need to fret," he added. "It's completely—"

CRACK!

Little Rock's foot broke through the ice!

Everyone froze, afraid that even the slightest movement would cause the crack to grow. Their eyes darted around, looking for a way to safety. Anna saw that the riverbank behind them was close enough to reach, but they still had no way to cross the dangerous river.

Suddenly, the ice shattered beneath Little Rock's feet! Anna and Kristoff grabbed him a moment before he fell through to the icy cold water. They struggled to hold his heavy body up. Anna's mind raced as she tried to figure out what to do next. "Elsa!" she called. "Maybe a stairway can get us across?"

Recalling the story she and Anna had

shared, Elsa quickly waved her arms through the air. A swirl of icy magic rose up above them. It curved and twisted until it formed a stairway made of ice, arching across the river like a bridge!

For a moment, everyone stared in awe at the elegant staircase. It looked as if an artist had spent years chiseling every inch of it, perfecting each curve and step.

"A little ornate for a rescue, no?" said Anna.

Elsa shrugged. "I guess my staircases have improved over the years."

Everyone scrambled up onto the riverbank and made their way toward the staircase. They began climbing up as gently and quickly as possible.

But once they made it to the very top of the arch—*CRACK!* The riverbank beneath the staircase began to crumble!

Little Rock looked at everyone helplessly. "What should we do?" he cried.

As the riverbank cracked into pieces, the staircase began to sway. It was only a matter of time before it fell into the frozen river.

"Wow," said Olaf. "What a delightful wobble!"

Without a second to lose, Elsa waved her arms again and another swirl of icy magic appeared, as if rising from the earth. This time, six ice sleds formed, one beside each of them. "Jump on!" she shouted.

As the staircase began to teeter to one side,

everyone leapt onto a sled. They swooshed across the steep arch and slid onto the frozen river.

They hooted and hollered as their sleds raced across the ice, picking up more and more speed.

"Woooo-hoooo!" Little Rock wore a giant smile across his face. He had never been on such an exhilarating ride!

"This is the best ride ever!" cried Olaf.

They picked up so much speed that the momentum carried them forward even after they reached the bottom. They continued to glide across the frozen river!

CHAPTER 7

ONCE THE SLEDS SLOWED TO A STOP, everyone cheered. They had made it all the way to the other side of the mountain!

Little Rock smiled up at Elsa and Anna. "You saved us!" he said, getting off his sled to hug them. "Anna, you thought of that staircase so fast. And, Elsa, you didn't hesitate with those ice sleds!" He looked at them with awe and appreciation. "Both of you are fearless!"

Little Rock reached for his pouch and loosened the string. He removed one of the glowing crystals, held it up, and said, "I want to share my ice crystal with you because you fearlessly faced the ice." He handed it to them.

The girls were so touched by Little Rock's gesture. How generous and kind to share his hard-earned crystal with them! They thanked him and each gave him a big hug.

Anna held the crystal tightly. "We'll take good care of it for you," she said. "Until you need it for the ceremony." She smiled and placed the crystal in her pocket.

When the group came upon another split

in the path, Little Rock was ready to take charge. He wanted to be fearless like Elsa and Anna. He took a deep breath and without a second thought started down the middle path.

Kristoff cleared his throat and whispered, "That's back to the river."

Little Rock turned on his heel and marched down the other path, refusing to let the mistake spoil his moment. "This way!" he declared.

Before long, the sun began to scare off the night sky. Little Rock yawned.

"We'd better stop and rest since trolls

usually sleep during the day," said Kristoff. "What do you think, Little Rock?"

"I think that's probably a good idea," he said, letting out another big yawn. "If you're all tired, too."

Anna pointed to a clearing off the path and suggested they might find a good place in that direction. Everyone agreed. They had been trekking for a long time. They walked to the clearing and found a perfect spot alongside a little brook. The open area felt warmer and more comfortable than the rocky mountains and hills nearby. Big spruce and pine trees surrounded the clearing, and the faint babble of the brook was as delightful and calming as a lullaby.

As soon as Little Rock sat down near a moss-covered tree trunk, he rolled up into a ball and went to sleep. He looked just like any other rock on the ground.

Elsa and Anna pulled Kristoff aside for a quiet conversation.

"We don't want to upset Little Rock," said Anna. "But shouldn't we be concerned? We only have two more nights and then . . . it's over."

"I guess we're just a bit worried," explained Elsa. "What if he misses the ceremony?"

"What if we can't find Grand Pabbie?" added Anna. "Or what if we find him and get there in time for the ceremony, but Little Rock doesn't have his tracking crystal glowing?"

Kristoff understood their concern. "Well, if he misses the ceremony or doesn't earn his crystal, he'll have to wait until next year." He shook his head. "It would crush him."

Anna and Elsa nodded. They could only imagine how sad Little Rock would be if he were to get left back after being so close. He was trying so hard, and they really wanted him to make it. But they also knew that wanting something wasn't enough and worrying wouldn't do any good.

"I guess all we can do is keep going," said Anna.

"And support him," added Elsa. "We'll be ready to leave as soon as he wakes up."

They decided that they all needed to rest.

The mountain range was vast, and there was no way of knowing how close they were to the end of their journey.

Kristoff and Elsa quickly fell asleep while Anna took a little time to write in her journal. Before she was able to finish her last sentence, she closed her eyes and drifted off to sleep.

CHAPTER 8

AS THE SUN STARTED DOWN THE SKY, painting it shades of pink and orange, Little Rock uncurled from his rock form. Still half asleep and groggy, he mumbled, "Don't take my toadstool. No, I want it and it looks crunchy." Then his eyes popped open. He wiped the drool from his mouth and sat up. He noticed his sleeping friends and the mountainside around him. It took him a moment to recall where he was and what he was doing. Once it registered, he felt a jolt of excitement. He sprang into the air, landed with a loud thud, and cheerfully sang, "It's wake-up time, everybody!"

Olaf appeared on a nearby trail and came running over when he heard the sound of Little Rock's voice.

"Hi, Little Rock!" Olaf exclaimed.

Little Rock smiled. He was surprised to see that Olaf was already awake. But as he stared at the snowman, he realized that something looked different about him. He just wasn't sure what it was.

"I was too excited to sleep, so I went

exploring!" Olaf explained. He told Little Rock that he had wandered through the mountainside. "It's amazing up here!" he exclaimed. "There are so many things to see. I was walking around and found this really shiny green bug! It flew right in front of my face. I was so surprised that my arms fell right off! But then I only found one arm. . . . I'm sure the other one will turn up somewhere."

"That's what's different!" Little Rock realized. "Maybe we can track your arm!" he said, eager to start exploring. "Did you see any signs of Grand Pabbie anywhere?"

"I don't think so. . . . I wonder if Grand Pabbie saw that bug, too," Olaf said.

Little Rock couldn't wait any longer. He

turned to the slumbering group, ready to take charge. "The sun is going to sleep, so it's time to wake up and get tracking, everyone!" he announced.

"That just sounds so wrong," said Anna, trying very hard to open her eyes.

"It's the troll way," Kristoff said, rising with a yawn.

"Good morning—I mean, evening," said Elsa, stretching her arms high above her head.

"Good evening," said Anna, smiling sleepily as she sat up.

"That's right," said Little Rock as he walked on top of a thick tree root, trying to balance, carefully placing one foot in front of the other. "We say good morning when we go

to sleep and good evening when we wake up."
He tried to follow the root's maze-like path
across the ground. "You guys make excellent
trolls."

Anna and Elsa chuckled and thanked Little
Rock for the compliment. Slowly following
Kristoff's lead, Anna knelt by the brook and
cupped her hands. Then she scooped up
some cold water and splashed it on her face.
She shrieked as the icy water touched her
skin. "Cold!" she yelped.

"Brrrrr!" Kristoff's lips made a funny noise
as he shook his head, spraying water droplets
all around him. "Yes, but it's instant energy,"
he said, looking at her. His face was a rosy
shade of red. "Right?"

She had to agree. The fresh, cool water was definitely helping her wake up.

"Everybody ready to start tracking?" asked Little Rock. Once the group pulled themselves together, they started toward the path. "This way!" he shouted, once again leading them.

The mountain trail was lined with towering spruce and pine trees that had dropped heavy pinecones. There were tons of them scattered on the ground. Anna picked one up to admire its beauty and was surprised by its weight.

"Catch!" she called to Kristoff, tossing it to him.

"Whoa," he said as he caught it, feeling its weight in his hands. "They really are giant." Kristoff tossed the pinecone to Little Rock.

The troll happily caught it with one hand.

"They're also very useful," said Little Rock, running the pinecone through his sprouts of hair. "They make great combs." He brought the pinecone to his back and moved it up and down. "Excellent back scratchers. *And* they're surprisingly delicious." He opened his mouth wide and threw the pinecone in! Everyone watched in awe as he crunched down on it. In a few bites, it was gone. "That was good," said Little Rock. "Thanks."

Sven curiously nudged a pinecone and licked it. He winced and tried to rid himself of the terrible flavor.

"So," said Kristoff, walking beside Little Rock. "Which tracking rule are you going to try tonight?" He really wanted to help Little Rock tap into his skills. "What do you think you should do?"

Little Rock scratched his chin and twisted his mouth to one side as he thought hard. "Be fearless, be observant, be inventive," he muttered under his breath, counting on his fingers to make sure he had thought of all three tracking rules. "I think I'll work on being observant. I'm going to look for clues."

"Excellent," said Kristoff. "Great idea."

Wearing a serious expression, Little Rock scanned the immediate area. "And I shall leave no shrub unturned," he said, holding up a finger. He scurried over to a nearby bush and peeked under it, but there was nothing there but a small squirrel guarding a nut. As they walked, he inspected the bark of trees and saw only tiny bugs. He looked up in the tree branches and at the sky, but saw only birds. He even picked up a rock and looked underneath it, but he saw only some fat worms wiggling their way into the earth.

Then Little Rock saw something sticking out next to a boulder. He gasped. "I see a clue," he announced, hustling over and lifting up the object to show everyone his great discovery: a broken tree branch.

"Grand Pabbie must have gone this way!" he said, pointing in the same direction as the branch.

Olaf's eyes went wide as he rushed over

waving a twig arm. "There you are, Arm!" he said gleefully to the branch.

The branch moved, waving back at Olaf! It startled Little Rock and caused him to drop it on the ground. Olaf picked it up and stuck it back onto his body, adjusting it until it fit just right. "Ah," he said, pleased. "That is so much better. Thanks, Little Rock!"

Kristoff noticed Little Rock's look of disappointment. "Now, that's a mistake that could have happened to any troll," he said. "And you helped Olaf. Imagine how he would have felt if he had left his arm up here on this mountain forever."

Little Rock's eyes brightened. "You're right," he said. "That would have been terrible. I'm glad I found your arm, Olaf."

"You're a really good tracker," said Olaf, thanking him again.

Upon hearing this compliment, an idea came to Little Rock's mind and he reached for his pouch. He quickly loosened the string and peeked inside, searching for his tracking crystal.

But it was still as dull as it had been when they left Troll Valley. Little Rock turned to Kristoff and showed him the crystal. "I thought maybe finding Olaf's arm would cause my crystal to glow," he said.

Kristoff knelt down next to Little Rock and put his hand on the sad little troll's shoulder. "It was a good try, but finding Olaf's arm was an accident—you thought it could be a clue to Grand Pabbie," he said gently. "You just have to keep trying. I'm sure you'll find a real clue somewhere."

Little Rock knew Kristoff was right—he had to keep going. He tied up the pouch and secured it again. He looked at the gang, forcing a smile. "Well, we'd better keep going," he said. "I'm being observant, so I know there could be an important clue right around the bend." Everyone was impressed. Despite the bumps along the way, Little Rock was doing a great job of remaining optimistic.

As they continued to walk up the mountain, fewer and fewer trees lined the path and the sky grew darker. There were no Northern

Lights, much to the group's disappointment, but the stars illuminated the night sky with their bright, twinkling lights..

"I don't think I've ever seen so many stars," said Anna, appreciating the view.

"It's really beautiful," said Elsa.

"Hey—the stars sleep during the day and wake up and sparkle at night. Just like you, Little Rock!" Olaf added.

Little Rock chuckled. He had never been compared to a star before.

"I did earn my stargazing crystal," he said. "So I can tell you that right there is the North Star." He pointed to a radiant star in the sky.

Everyone listened as Little Rock continued to point out some of the other stars he knew.

He even showed them several constellations. "That's the Great Granite Hare," he explained, pointing to a cluster of stars in the shape of a rabbit. "See its ears?" "And that one over there is the Fox." He pointed to the fox shape behind the Hare. "See how it looks like the Fox is chasing the rabbit?" Little Rock giggled. "He's right behind him but he'll never ever catch him." The group was impressed with Little Rock's knowledge of stars. "I like them because they are pictures in the sky that tell stories," he added.

As they continued to walk, Little Rock told them about some of the other constellations and the stories that went along with them. But when something on the ground distracted him, he became very excited. "Hey!" he said, calling everyone over. "I've found something really important! A clue!"

He held up a thick piece of bright green moss. "It's from Grand Pabbie's cloak!" he exclaimed. He turned the piece of moss ever so slightly, using the starlight to see as he inspected it from every angle. "Yup. I'd know it anywhere."

Olaf took a step closer to Little Rock to check out the moss and felt something on his foot. "Look!" he shouted, holding up his foot to show a bunch of moss dangling from it. "I have a clue, too!"

Elsa didn't want to hurt their feelings, but she pointed out that there was moss covering much of the surrounding area. "It's possible that it's not from Grand Pabbie's cloak. It could just be . . . moss."

Little Rock looked around and saw that Elsa was right. Moss was growing alongside the path and *on* the path—it was everywhere. In fact, it wasn't just Olaf who had some stuck to his foot—they all did! Even Sven had some stringy pieces of the soft moss tangled around his hooves. It stretched up from the ground as he grunted and stomped his legs, trying to get it off.

Little Rock sighed and nodded his head. "You are correct, Elsa," he said. "This is *not* from Grand Pabbie's cloak. This is just moss." He tossed it over his shoulder and wiped his hands together, shaking off the dirt and preparing to move on.

Olaf followed Little Rock's lead and did the same. "It's just moss," he said, holding it up, about to toss it aside. "But very beautiful moss." He dropped it gently back to the ground.

"Well, I guess we'd better keep going," said Little Rock, refusing to get discouraged. He continued to march up the mountain, with his friends following close behind.

CHAPTER 9

As they walked, the moss became sparse, and soon the ground was covered with snow that glittered in the starlight.

The higher they climbed, the chillier it became, until the snow was deep enough to hug their ankles. It was a cold reminder that winter was only a couple of days away. That brought one important question to everyone's mind: would they find Grand Pabbie in time for the ceremony? Nobody wanted to ask the question aloud, so they continued to walk silently, hoping they would find even a tiny clue very soon.

Near the top of the mountain and just off the trail, Anna and Kristoff noticed some interesting tracks in the snow.

"Those look like Grand Pabbie's, don't they?" Anna whispered. Kristoff took one look at the chunky troll prints and nodded.

"Little Rock!" he called. "Come check these out."

But Little Rock was busy. He had found some interesting tracks, too—only his were on the path.

"Hold on, Kristoff," he called back. "I have a real clue over here: tracks! They could be Grand Pabbie's." He eagerly followed the tracks. "This could be the clue I've been looking for! This could be the thing that finally leads us to—"

He stopped talking as the tracks came to an end, leading him to . . .

"Sven?" he said, disappointed. The rcindeer looked at him and seemed to smile, then gave him a big lick across the cheek. Little Rock sighed and patted Sven on the head. Then he turned around and walked off the trail, into a little clearing. "How could I be so wrong?" He lookcd up at the sky and shouted, "How? Every single time!" Then he groaned dramatically and fell backward into the deep snow, gazing up at the sky.

"Little Rock," said Kristoff, trying not to laugh. "You really should come look at these prints over here." But Little Rock didn't budge. He just lay there on the ground, staring at the stars.

Anna walked over to him and offered him her hand. "Come on," she said. "We need you to look at them to see what you think. You're the tracker *and* you know Grand Pabbie best. You're the expert here."

He looked up at her and couldn't help it—a smile slowly crept across his face. He knew he was acting silly throwing himself into the snow like that. He reached up and grabbed her hand. She tried to help pull him up, but he slipped, causing them both to fall!

"Sorry, Anna!" Little Rock cried.

They sat up and looked at each other, their heads covered in snow. All they could do was laugh.

"Maybe we'd both better just get up on our own," Anna said.

Little Rock bounced right up, landing on his feet, and put his hand out toward Anna. "*I'll* help *you*," he said. Anna smiled and grabbed his hand, and he pulled her up.

Anna led Little Rock over to the tracks she and Kristoff had found. "So?" she asked. "What do you think?"

Little Rock inspected the footprints.

"Could they belong to Grand Pabbie?" asked Kristoff.

Little Rock knelt beside the tracks and sniffed them. He traced his finger in the snow around them. Then he looked at them from different angles, framing them with his hands, as if trying to size them up. He placed a foot beside one of the tracks and pushed into the snow. He compared the prints, twisting up his face as if thinking with all his might.

Finally, he looked at Kristoff and Anna with his eyebrows raised. "These are Grand Pabbie's footprints!" he announced. "This way, everyone!" Little Rock followed the tracks up a steep incline.

But when they got to the very top, they saw

something odd: the footprints stopped at the end of a narrow, rocky cliff.

"What happened?" asked Little Rock, lost in thought. "This can't be good." His voice quavered with worry. He talked rapidly as he paced, imagining what terrible things might have befallen Grand Pabbie. "A giant bird could have swooped onto the mountain and picked him up in its giant talons." He grew more and more anxious. "Or a squirrel might have mistaken Grand Pabbie for a delicious nut!"

"Little Rock," said Kristoff, trying to interrupt his worrying.

"Or maybe it was a big swarm of angry butterflies!" said Little Rock, unable to stop himself. "They could have just gobbled him up without leaving a trace!"

"Little Rock!" said Kristoff, demanding his attention. "I'm sure Grand Pabbie is fine. None of those things happened."

"How do you know?" asked Little Rock.

"Well," started Kristoff. "Let's see. . . . There are no birds strong enough to pick up Grand Pabbie. He's pretty heavy, remember? And squirrels are friendly toward trolls. You guys are good friends. There's no way a squirrel would mistake a troll for a nut. Plus, trolls are too big to be nuts. And butterflies— even when they're angry—prefer pollen. Not trolls."

Little Rock smiled and a giggle escaped his

lips. He realized how ridiculous he sounded. "Okay, you're right. Maybe my imagination went a little wild there for a minute."

"Just a little," said Kristoff playfully.

But Anna, who had been looking up at the sky, wore a worried expression.

"Look at that," she said, pointing. A big, dark cloud had caused a cluster of stars to go dim. The cloud appeared to be getting bigger by the second.

"Looks like a storm is coming," said Kristoff.

Little Rock frowned. "Nah," he said. "Just a passing cloud. We'll be okay. Let's not worry about it. I'm done worrying about things. I think I'm going to start a fourth rule of tracking: Don't worry about things. What do you guys think?"

"That sounds like a great rule," said Olaf.

"When we find Grand Pabbie, I'll talk to him about adding it," said Little Rock.

The wind suddenly picked up and whistled through the tall, thin birch trees. Their branches swayed as the last leaves of autumn tore off and scattered about.

Soon the stars completely disappeared. It was as if the giant cloud had devoured them, making them vanish. A heavy blanket covered the sky, and the whole mountain looked ominous as the wind began to howl, getting louder and stronger with every second.

Little Rock turned to the group. "You

know, I think you may be right," he said. The wind whipped through his little sprouts of hair, bending them flat against his head. "I think there's a good chance that a storm is coming." Everyone agreed. They knew they had to do something fast. "I'm feeling a lot more experienced in my traveling and exploring. You guys stay here and I'll go find shelter," said Little Rock.

"NO!" they all shouted.

"Let me try," offered Elsa. "I think I can help."

Everyone huddled together, protecting each other as the storm continued to build. The snow started falling so hard, the group could barely see each other.

Elsa waved her arms, and her icy magic swirled around them. She continued until an ice shelter magically grew from the earth, shielding them on all sides. The ice sculpture was curved at the top, and thick enough to keep them safe as the blizzard began to rage outside. It was like being inside a beautiful dome of ice.

"Good thinking, Elsa," said Anna. "It's so snug and cozy in here."

"We may be here for a while," said Kristoff. "Seems pretty rough out there."

"Hey," said Little Rock. "How about another story? Anyone have one to share?"

Olaf raised a twig arm. "Oooh, I do!" he said. "This storm reminds me of a story I know. And it's about the Northern Lights! Do you want to hear it?"

Everyone agreed: it was the perfect time for Olaf to tell his story. The snowman smiled and began.

CHAPTER 10

OLAF: Okay. On a very cold, very snowy night, Elsa built me with her magic on top of a very cold, very snowy mountain: the North Mountain!

I opened my eyes, and I couldn't believe it—I could see stuff! And I said, "Hi. I'm Olaf, and I like warm hugs." I could talk! It was wonderful! Oh, I remember it so well.

Then I moved! I turned my head, I tilted it, I looked up and down and spun it all the way around. I moved my left leg, and then I moved my right leg. Oh! And I wiggled my butt. Side to side like this . . . and back to front like this . . . Then I spun it all the way around like this. It was like dancing!

It was the best thing ever. For the first time, I had these amazing moving parts. And then after all that moving and wiggling, something else happened: I WALKED! I could actually go places!

So I just started walking and

exploring. I wanted to see it all—everything was so beautiful! There was no one else around, but there was snow . . . and air . . . and ice . . . and snow . . . and stars . . . and the moon . . . oh—and snow.

We saw a lot of snow today. And now with the blizzard blowing out there, I'm sure we're going to see even more. I love the summer and the sun, but I love winter and snow, too. Snow is always so white and fluffy and soft. Wouldn't it be fun if it were a different color once in a while? Green like the grass, maybe. Or pink like a flower. All happy, warm colors so it could be like summer all year round!

Soooo, where was I? Oh, right! So I was moving around, exploring, and having a great time as I went down the North Mountain—which was really big and steep. As I started walking down, my legs kept moving faster and faster, and before I knew it, I was running! Soon I was going so fast that I slipped and started to tumble. Everything was all crazy and swirling around and around and around and around. It was like my life was upside down! I was going so fast that I lost my head. And my legs. And my butt. And my middle. Everything was rolling down the mountain in all different directions! I loved it!

Oooh. Wow. That wind is loud, isn't it? It sounds a little angry. Like it could really use a nice warm hug. It was windy on the North Mountain that night, too, but it wasn't this loud. I love this cozy shelter. Thanks for building it, Elsa.

So, back to my story. I'm tumbling down the mountain in pieces—*whooooopeee!*—having a great time watching the world spin by, and some of my parts collected things along the way. A couple of branches got stuck in my middle, and my butt picked up some of these little round things . . . and a few twigs got stuck in my legs.

When all of me got to the bottom and stopped, I looked around and wondered how I would get myself together. But then I saw those branches stuck in my middle and put them on either side—they were actually my arms! And they worked! So I gathered all my parts in one place and tried to fit everything together. Since it was only my first day, it took me a while. I put my butt on my head; then my head was on upside down. I tried my middle on the side, then on the top. I tried a bunch of different things, but nothing felt right.

Then this big gray bird swooped down and landed right near me. I looked at it, and I could see how his head went on top, so I tried that. I put it on just like his. Then I noticed the bird's legs and stuck my two legs on the bottom.

I pulled those round things off my butt and put them down the front. See? Right here. Buttons! They looked great. Oh, and I put the twig on my head—it gave me hair! Only first, I had it on my forehead; then I tried it by my ear. I tried it on as a nose, but that didn't work, either. I didn't get my nose that day. That came from Anna. So anyway, it took me a little while, but when I put the twig on the very top of my head, it felt just right. Now I was perfect!

Then the bird flew into the sky. I watched it fly away and suddenly I saw this bright green light appear. I thought the bird was doing it! But no, it was the Northern Lights! The green light grew and grew, slowly swirling around the stars and the moon—it was like a super-slow wiggle! And it kept growing and growing. The sky was awake, like me! I just stared, watching it move. I had never seen anything so beautiful before. Sure, I had only been alive for a few minutes, but it was the best day of my life! Soon the green light seemed to cover half the sky. I watched it all night long. Now anytime I see the Northern Lights dancing and swirling in the sky, I think about that day and how I felt so happy to be part of such a beautiful world.

CHAPTER 11

"Wow," said Little Rock. "That was a great story, Olaf!" He loved listening to his new friends tell their tales.

Suddenly, Little Rock's ears twitched and he held up a hand. "Shhhh. Wait," he whispered. "Listen."

As everyone quieted, they could hear what Little Rock heard—or rather, what he didn't hear. There was silence. The storm outside had stopped howling and beating against the walls of the shelter. "No more wind," said Little Rock. "The storm must be over!"

Olaf peeked outside and announced that Little Rock was correct—the blizzard had passed. The remaining clouds sailed across the sky, revealing the moon and stars. Everything was calm.

Little Rock stepped over a mound of snow at the entrance to the shelter and took in his surroundings. "Wow," he said. "That's a lot of snow. The mountain is *covered*! Everything looks so different."

The group followed him out and gazed at the wintry wonderland. The fresh, powdery snow was a shade of blue in the dim moonlight, and it seemed to go on forever. Dripping icicles hung from tree branches like beautiful crystal ornaments.

Everyone moved slowly. With each step, their feet sank, making it difficult to walk.

"So what should we do next?" asked Kristoff, trudging through the deep drifts. "Little Rock?" He turned to see Little Rock on all fours.

"If I do it *really* gently, maybe it will work," said Little Rock, sifting through the snow.

"Um . . . what are you trying to do?" asked Anna, awkwardly pulling a leg up and attempting to take another step.

"Dig up Grand Pabbie's footprints," he said. "Right before the storm hit, we were following them, and if I can get to them, we can keep going and find Grand Pabbie."

"The tracks ended here at the top of the cliff, remember?" Kristoff said.

"Oops," said Little Rock, getting up off the ground. "I forgot about that part." He smiled shyly. "I guess I was just so excited about that clue. That was a really good one."

"It was," said Kristoff. "And we can still use it." He knocked some snow off his pants. "Let's think."

"Right," agreed Little Rock. "Let's think. Grand Pabbie was up here—we know that. So where could he have gone next?" He scanned the area.

"Maybe he went down the other side of the mountain," suggested Elsa. "We should head that way. There could be another clue for us to find."

"I bet that's exactly what he did," said Little Rock. "Let's go!"

The group slowly made their way over to the cliff and looked below. The moon gave off enough light to illuminate the huge drop and the steep mountainside covered in smooth, untouched snow. Stunned, they gazed silently at the snowy stretch, trying to figure out their next move.

Suddenly, an idea popped into Little Rock's head. He turned to Olaf. "Hey! Remember your story?"

"Uh-huh. Yes, I remember," Olaf said.

"Could we do that?" asked the troll.

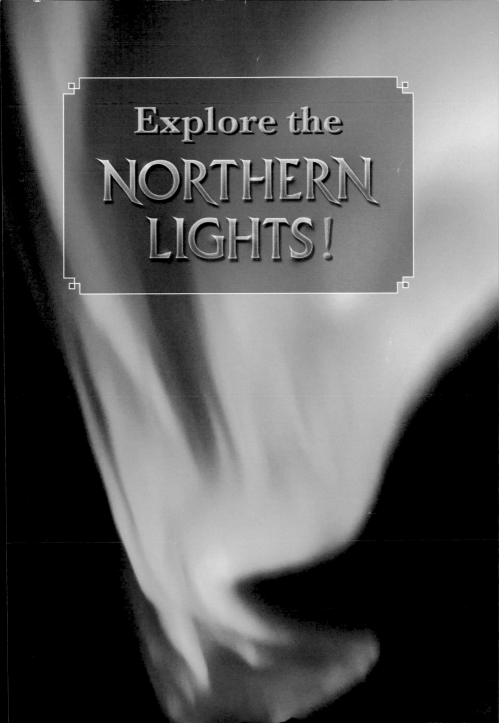

Explore the
NORTHERN
LIGHTS!

The Northern Lights

The Northern Lights (also called the aurora borealis) are colorful lights in the night sky. They form when tiny particles from the sun bump into the gases that are all around Earth. When these particles and gases crash into each other, they create the colorful lights.

Locations

The Northern Lights mostly appear near the Arctic Circle. This includes the northern parts of Alaska, Canada, Greenland, Iceland, Norway, Sweden, Finland, and Russia.

 In Anna and Elsa's time, scientists were just beginning to understand the Northern Lights. They discovered that Earth's magnetic field affected particles in the air.

An aerial view of the Arctic Circle

Seasons

Autumn and winter are the best seasons to see the Northern Lights. During this time, the weather is often cold and snowy. If you take a trip to see the Northern Lights, be sure to bundle up!

CONDITIONS

If you look up at the sky on a clear, dark night, you should be able to see stars. The Northern Lights are like stars because they can only be seen at night when the sky is dark and cloudless. Bright cities make it more difficult to see the Northern Lights, so it's often better to watch them in rural areas. People use snowshoes, snowmobiles, dog sleds, and even reindeer sleighs to travel to the best spots for viewing the colorful lights.

For people in Arendelle, a journey to see the Northern Lights was very special. They prepared for days, and were eager to begin the adventure.

Colors and Shapes

The Northern Lights can be many different colors. Sometimes the lights look like a rainbow, and other times they are only one color. Green and yellow are the most common colors, and violet and red are the rarest. The lights can also look like different shapes and patterns, such as waves, stripes, or spirals.

Movement

Sometimes the Northern Lights look like they are dancing or rolling in the sky. This movement is caused by sudden changes in energy in the atmosphere. When these changes happen, the lights put on an amazing show!

In the time of *Frozen*, people could only see the Northern Lights in person or if the lights were shown in paintings. They couldn't take photographs of the lights like we can today.

Olaf gasped and nodded. He knew exactly what Little Rock meant. "I *love* that idea!" he said with a giggle. Then he dove over the side of the mountain! "See ya at the bottom!" he called as he tumbled down, his body parts rolling across the mountain in multiple directions.

Little Rock curled up so that he looked like a big, mossy rock and rolled down the mountain, speeding after Olaf.

"Well?" said Kristoff, looking at Elsa and Anna. "What do you think?"

They looked over the mountainside, gauging whether they were willing to follow.

"It beats walking," said Anna, her feet sinking deep into the snow. "Last one down is leftover lutefisk!" she yelled, and leapt over the ledge, sliding and laughing all the way!

"Oh no you don't!" said Kristoff, flinging himself onto the mountainside and speeding toward her.

"Wait for me!" said Elsa as she joined in the fun.

Sven hopped off the ridge and slid down on his backside. He caught up to Olaf's head on the way down. "Hi, Sven," said Olaf's head cheerfully as it rolled by.

It was a long ride down the mountainside, and the friends enjoyed every second, racing each other all the way to the bottom.

CHAPTER 12

ONCE HE STOPPED, LITTLE ROCK uncurled himself and popped back open. "That was fun!" he exclaimed.

"It was so much fun!" agreed Olaf. "We should do it again!"

Little Rock looked at Olaf. His head was on the ground and he was looking up with a wide smile stretched across his face. Olaf appeared to be buried in the snow up to his neck! It took Little Rock a second to realize it was just Olaf's head, and he stood and helped collect the snowman's scattered parts.

"Here's your middle," he announced as he carried it over. "Hey, and where's your nose?"

Olaf looked down, trying to see if his nose was actually gone. He hadn't noticed. "Oh, Nosey! Where did you get to?" he called.

Little Rock turned to see Sven with Olaf's nose in his mouth. Sven smiled and dropped the carrot onto the snow as a big string of drool dripped down his lips. Olaf reached for the carrot and stuck it back on his face . . . along with a little drool.

"Thanks, Sven!" said Olaf.

Little Rock found Olaf's other parts and helped Olaf put himself back together again.

"Thank you, Little Rock," said Olaf, putting his legs back onto his bottom.

"Here's an arm," said Little Rock, pushing it into Olaf's middle.

When Elsa, Anna, and Kristoff reached the bottom and finally slowed to a stop, they were still laughing. Their stomachs ached from laughing so hard, and they had to take a minute to catch their breath.

"I'd call it a tie," said Anna. Then she collapsed backward and made a snow angel. She simply couldn't resist with all that fresh, powdery snow. Elsa joined her, and the two sisters lay next to each other for a moment, gazing up at the sparkling night sky. The moon was a sliver that looked like a smile high above them.

Little Rock stood up and cleared his throat. "Olaf," he said, holding his crystal pouch and loosening the string, "you deserve to carry a crystal."

Olaf gasped. He couldn't believe he was receiving such an honor!

Little Rock removed a glowing crystal from his pouch and held it out to Olaf. "I'm going to lend you my snow crystal because you gave me that great idea with your story."

Olaf beamed as he took the crystal. "Thank you so much. It's beautiful!" he exclaimed, holding it up against his cheek. "It's shinier than that green bug I found." He gave Little Rock a warm hug and thanked him again.

Kristoff smiled proudly at Little Rock. "That was very observant of you, Little Rock," he said. "You realized that Olaf's story was an effective way to get down that steep mountain. Well done."

Little Rock grinned. It felt great to have done something right.

Then a low rumbling sounded from above. "Sven? Please tell me that was your stomach," said Kristoff.

The ground trembled beneath their feet, and the noise resounded around the area. Kristoff looked up at the mountain peak and his eyes went wide.

"Avalanche!" he yelled. "RUN!"

Without looking back, the friends sprinted as fast as they could, but the deep snow became like anchors weighing down every step they made. Anna spotted a large, rocky overhang jutting out of the mountain and gestured toward it.

"That way!" she shouted. "Everyone get beneath the overhang!"

As chunks of ice crumbled and snow rained down, the friends huddled close together underneath the slab of rock and braced themselves for the worst. As the avalanche slid closer, they could hear it getting louder and louder!

But a moment before it reached the

overhang, the avalanche petered out. A light dusting of snow shot over the rocky ledge and delicately sprinkled down in front of their faces. Then three little snowballs rolled alongside the overhang and stacked one on top of the other, creating a miniature snowman. Olaf scratched a smile into the head with his finger and said, "Hello, Mr. Avalanche." He turned to the group. "He's not so scary."

They all laughed with relief.

"Olaf," said Anna. "Where is your crystal?"

Olaf turned in a circle as he looked all around him. "Oh no! Where's Little Rock's snow crystal? Oh no, oh no, oh no!"

Anna noticed a glimmer in the center of Olaf's back as he turned away from her. She smiled and plucked it off him. "Found it! Must have happened while you were running from the avalanche."

"Oh, phew! Thanks, Snow," said Olaf, patting his middle appreciatively.

Anna asked if he'd like her to keep the crystal safe for him, and he was very happy with that idea. She tucked it into her pocket along with the ice crystal.

"Wow," said Elsa, pointing out the crack of sunlight that was starting to rise over the horizon. "With all that excitement, I totally lost track of time."

"Me too," said Anna.

"We should probably— Wait, where's Little Rock?" asked Kristoff.

"Oh, he's right here," Olaf whispered as he looked down at Little Rock, who had rolled up into a ball next to him. "Maybe this is the perfect place for a nap," he added. "Isn't he sweet when he's asleep?"

They agreed to set up camp right there, under the overhang. Before going to sleep, Anna asked Kristoff and Elsa to write in the journal. She thought it would give it a more well-rounded perspective if it included different points of view. So they each took a turn with the pencil, jotting down just a few things.

Anna wrapped herself in her cloak, trying to keep warm as she waited for them to finish. They could have written about their adventures for hours, but they knew they needed their rest.

The overhang did a good job of blocking out the sun, but Elsa, Anna, and Kristoff had trouble falling asleep. Their minds were heavy with thoughts, and they were all concerned about the same thing: winter was quickly on its way. They had to find Grand Pabbie before the next sunrise or it would be too late.

"The moon is already up!" shouted Little Rock as his eyes opened wide. He couldn't believe they had slept past sunset. He could tell by the light and the position of the moon that it wasn't *that* late, but they had definitely slept longer than he had planned. He quickly roused everyone. "Let's go, let's go, let's go!" he cheered. "Last night of autumn!"

The group started walking along the lower mountain trail. Little Rock looked down at the pristine, smooth snow. Why hadn't they found any more signs of Grand Pabbie? Then he had an idea: if there was nothing above the snow, maybe there was something underneath.

"Wait! I think I may be able to find a clue!" he announced to the group.

He knelt down in the snow and began digging. He continued digging deeper and deeper until only his little feet were sticking out. After a few seconds, he popped up holding a bunch of rope in one hand and an ice pick in another.

"Look what I found!" he cried. "These must have belonged to Grand Pabbie!"

"I think those are mine," Kristoff said as he inspected Little Rock's discoveries. "I was wondering where they went!"

"Oh, well, here you go," Little Rock murmured as he handed the items to Kristoff. He thought he was so close to finding a clue.

"It's okay," said Kristoff. "I'm grateful that you found my things." He placed the rope and ice pick in Sven's saddlebag. "Let's keep walking. I'm sure we'll find another clue soon."

As they continued, Little Rock thought about the quest. He knew he had to earn the tracking crystal *and* find Grand Pabbie before the end of the night in order to be in the ceremony. Kristoff and everyone had helped him so much that he wanted to succeed for them, too.

He thought about how disappointed they would all be if they missed the ceremony or if he didn't get his crystal to glow. They were trying so hard to help him. If he failed, he would be letting them down. He just *had* to get this right.

Determined, Little Rock reviewed the rules of tracking in his mind and decided he should try to use the third one. He wondered whether he could do it—or if he even knew what it really meant.

"Be inventive," he muttered. "How do you do that?"

Kristoff smiled. It was the perfect time for him to share his favorite Northern Lights memory.

CHAPTER 13

KRISTOFF: One night, when I was just a kid, Sven and I were out harvesting ice from a frozen river. We would sell what we had off our sled during the day and then go out at night to get more.

It was cold, obviously, and pretty late. I was working on getting a big block of ice onto the sled. It was probably a bit larger than I should have cut, and I was having some trouble with it. Anyway, the Northern Lights were up there, glowing in the sky. We would see them pretty often, but this time they were really bright—a kind of crazy super-bright green. There was no moon, so they were clearer and brighter because of that, too.

But anyway, the ice was crystal clear, and those bright lights were reflected on its surface. And they were driving Sven crazy. He was chasing them, as the lights seemed to bounce from place to place. He'd run around and slap his hoof down on one of the reflected lights, thinking he had caught it—but then it would suddenly appear right next to him. He was going nuts, chasing after every spot of light he saw, romping across the ice trying to capture them.

This went on for a good while and ended when he finally caught one—with his tongue. When he tried to lift his tongue off the ice, it just stretched and stretched—it wouldn't budge. He was stuck.

The more he tried to get his

tongue off, the more stuck it seemed to become. I think his tongue grew that day from all the stretching. It probably gained an inch! Anyway, I left my block of ice and went over to try to help him.

First I grabbed him around the waist and tried pulling and yanking on him. But that didn't work. Then I grabbed his face and tried pushing him backward. That didn't work, either. Well, except to squish his nose in. He looked pretty funny. I tried for a while, pushing and pulling at different angles, but it was clear it just wasn't going to happen.

I had to come up with a better idea. I had to *be inventive.* So I sat there and thought for a minute while he looked up at me with these pleading eyes. "Please help me, Kristoff. Come on, do something! I'm your only friend," he seemed to say. The poor guy.

I started digging through my bag, hoping something would inspire me. Finally, it came to me.

"I have an idea!" I announced.

Unfortunately, I happened to pull my giant ice pick out of my bag just as I said this. You should have seen the look on Sven's face!

I don't think I've ever seen his eyes so big. He was looking at me like, "No, please, no, I need my tongue! How will I ever taste a carrot again?"

I promise that I didn't mean to scare him! I moved the big ice pick to get to the tiny one—it was no bigger than my finger. "Trust me," I said. He kept looking at me with those big, panicked eyes. "Trust me, buddy," I said again. Finally, he closed his eyes.

I knelt down next to him. He opened one eye the tiniest crack, but I could tell he was totally watching me. I used the little pick to carefully chip away around his tongue. I was really gentle. *Tap tap tap tap tap.*

I tapped until I was able to pluck this tiny little piece of ice right out of the ground. He popped his tongue with the ice still attached to it into his mouth. There it melted, and he drank down the water, licked his lips, and was free!

He gave me a big, icy cold, slobbery kiss, and we sat next to each other and . . . yeah, we hugged. We sat under those bright Northern Lights, enjoying the show together.

CHAPTER 14

LITTLE ROCK LAUGHED. "YOU GUYS all have such great stories about the Northern Lights. It makes me wish I had one of my own!"

"Don't worry, Little Rock," said Anna. "After the crystal ceremony, you'll have the best Northern Lights story!"

Little Rock hoped Anna was right. But

with the reminder of the ceremony, everyone picked up the pace.

As they walked on with Little Rock in the lead, the path started to narrow, and soon it curved tightly around the mountain.

"Be careful," said Kristoff.

"Be *really* careful," Little Rock said, echoing Kristoff's warning.

They walked single file, as the path was too narrow for anyone to walk side by side. Sven had to take it extra slow so as not to slip. When they made their way around a sharp corner, they heard a strange sound in thc near distance.

"What is that?" asked Little Rock, tilting his head to listen. "Is it the wind?"

"I don't know, but I think we're getting closer to it," said Elsa as she concentrated on navigating the narrow trail.

"Yeah, it's definitely getting louder," agreed Anna.

Even though he wasn't sure what he would face around the next corner, Little Rock continued to lead. "Be careful as you walk over here," he called back to them. "It's getting a little slippery." He gripped the trail tightly with his toes. "I wonder if that sound is—" Little Rock gasped as he turned another sharp corner. He stopped in his tracks, startled by a grand sight: it was a giant waterfall! "Water," he said, finishing his thought.

As they filed in, past the curve, they couldn't

help stopping to stare at the waterfall when it came into view. It was cold outside, but it wasn't nearly frigid enough to freeze the powerful white water that rushed down the rocky face of the mountain into a pool that collected at the bottom. It was an incredible sight!

"A waterfall!" Olaf shouted with glee. "I've always wanted to swim in a waterfall. Put my head under it and let it rush over my face . . ." He started to make his way toward it.

Anna held him back. "We, uh, have to look around," she said. "For clues and things. No time to swim."

Little Rock led everyone toward the base of the waterfall, and they immediately started scouting.

Something hanging off a small rocky ledge caught Anna's eye and she went over to investigate. "This looks like it could be Grand Pabbie's," she said, holding up a mossy cloak.

Everyone rushed over to check out the cloak and agreed with her—it *was* Grand Pabbie's!

"He must have found a way up," said Elsa, looking at the massive waterfall.

"But how could he have?" Little Rock asked, looking around and trying to come up with some possibilities. "And how will *we* get up there?"

"That's a good question," Kristoff said as he analyzed the surrounding area. The rocks next to the waterfall were too steep for Sven and too tall for Little Rock and Olaf to climb. They needed a creative solution—fast!

Elsa had an idea, but just before she shared it with the group, Little Rock pointed and cried, "Where's Sven going?"

The group turned to the waterfall just in time to see Sven disappearing behind it. They had no idea that the clever reindeer found a small opening behind the rushing water. He then tried to wedge his body through, but his antlers prevented him from getting all the way in. He twisted and turned his body, but it was no use: his antlers were stuck. He let out a loud groan, calling for Kristoff.

Kristoff followed Sven and helped him twist his antlers just the right way so he could back out. "You okay, buddy?" he asked.

Sven grunted. He was relieved to be free!

"How do you forget you have antlers?" Kristoff joked. Then he walked behind the waterfall and peered in through the opening, hoping Sven might have found a way up. "Nope. It's just a dead end." He gave Sven a scratch. "But it was a good idea."

Kristoff returned to the group, but Sven walked over to the waterfall and put his tongue in it.

"Thirsty, Sven?" Little Rock asked, giggling.

Sven grunted and stomped his hoof against the ground several times to get their attention. Then he did it again. "I guess he is," said Anna. "Really thirsty."

Kristoff took one look at Sven and knew what the reindeer was trying to do. "Sven is suggesting Elsa freeze the waterfall," he said. "Remember my story?"

Sven snorted in approval and grinned goofily. Everyone was impressed with his creative idea!

Elsa waved her arms and used her icy magic to freeze the waterfall! Suddenly, the white raging water was frozen solid and appeared to be a light shade of blue.

"Hmmm," Little Rock said. "Now what?" They stared up at the giant pillar of ice.

"We climb," said Kristoff matter-of-factly.

"We climb," said Anna. "Of course! Yes!

We climb." She positioned herself against the vertical ice and reached her arms up over her head. "All right! I've always wanted to do this! Let's go!"

Kristoff looked at Anna incredulously. "You won't make it up without equipment," he said.

"I can do it," said Anna. She jumped and grabbed an icicle that was jutting out of the waterfall. As her hands began to slip, she swung her legs forward and wrapped them around the icicle.

"You can do it . . . with proper equipment," said Kristoff. He took an ice ax and a pair of metal plates with spikes out of Sven's saddlebag. After he strapped the plates onto the bottom of his shoes, the spikes sank into the snow as he stood.

Anna sighed and dropped back to the ground. "That's too bad. I *so* wanted to try waterfall climbing," she said.

Kristoff removed another ax and a pair of spikes from the saddlebag. Everyone looked a little surprised that he had such gear with him.

"What kind of ice harvester would I be if I left home unprepared for ice climbing?" he said.

Once they were ready, Kristoff gave Anna a quick lesson.

Anna was super excited. "I'm ready! Let's do this!" she cried.

For extra safety, Kristoff tied the rope around both their waists in case one of them slipped. That way, one person could climb while the other stayed stationary.

Anna and Kristoff used their axes and spikes to dig into the ice as they began to scale the waterfall. They moved quickly but carefully.

"When we get to the top, we'll throw the rope down," Kristoff called to everyone watching below.

"Okay," Olaf said, calling back. "We'll be right here. We won't move."

"Be careful, Anna!" cried Elsa, keeping her eyes on her little sister.

"I totally got this," said Anna, striking the

ice with her ax and pulling herself up. "I'll see you up there!"

As they climbed side by side, Anna whispered to Kristoff, "So do you think we're close?"

"I hope so," said Kristoff. "We don't have much time. Tonight is the last night of autumn." Kristoff smiled as he watched Anna whack the ax into the ice and take another step. "You're doing great. I'll take the lead."

Anna watched as Kristoff climbed a few feet above her and then gave her the signal that it was her turn.

She dug the spikes on her shoes into the ice and took one step and then another. "Guess you're a good teacher," she said as she pulled herself up alongside him. "This is tougher than it looks."

Kristoff had been walking up ice since he was a kid. In fact, he looked just as natural scaling a frozen waterfall as he did walking on the ground.

Kristoff looked up. "We're almost there," he said.

"Oh, good." Anna swung the ax again. "Not that I couldn't do this all day. I'm pretty much a mountain woman now, right?" she joked.

Kristoff laughed. "Pretty much."

They continued climbing, and before they knew it, they had reached the top. Kristoff pulled himself over the edge and then helped Anna up.

Everyone cheered from down below, and Anna and Kristoff waved at them.

"We made it!" Anna shouted, jumping up and down. "Ouch. Okay, remove the spikes." She removed the metal from her shoes. Then she hugged Kristoff. "I mean, I knew we would make it, but—"

"You climbed a waterfall," Kristoff said. "Pretty amazing, right?"

Anna grinned with pride. "Whoa," she said, noticing the view behind them. It looked like they were standing on top of the world. Mountains stretched as far as the eye could see—Anna could even make out Arendelle in the distance!

"Not a bad view," said Kristoff. Then

he turned and shouted, "Incoming!" He dropped the rope down to Elsa and turned to Anna. "Let's just hope Oaken's rope is as strong as he says."

CHAPTER 15

ELSA CAUGHT THE ROPE AND fashioned a sling out of it to secure Sven. Then she turned to Olaf. "Are you ready?" she asked.

"Of course!" he replied. "This is going to be so much fun!"

Elsa lifted Olaf and sat him down on Sven's head, in between his antlers.

"Be sure to hold on to Sven's antler's,

Olaf," she said, checking that he was secure and balanced.

"Hi, Sven," said Olaf, patting him. "Thanks for letting me ride."

"Okay," Elsa shouted up. "They're on!"

Kristoff and Anna had wrapped the rope around a tree to make a sort of pulley, and now they gripped it tightly and dug their heels into the ground. They used all their strength to hoist up Sven and Olaf.

Olaf enjoyed the slow and steady ride, giggling and shouting "Wheeee!" all the way.

When they reached the top, Sven nodded and tossed Olaf to the ground. "That was amazing!" exclaimed Olaf. "It was even better than I expected!"

Kristoff and Anna helped Sven over the

edge. He gave them both a lick, very happy to be back on solid ground.

"All right," said Anna, shaking her arms and legs and stretching her body a bit, preparing for another pull.

Kristoff dropped the rope back down to Elsa, then turned toward Olaf and Anna. "Now you guys get ready. We're all going to have to pull really hard to get Little Rock up." He tied the other end of the rope around Sven.

Everyone got into place as Elsa prepared Little Rock.

Little Rock looked way up to the top of the waterfall. It was so high! He was a little worried about falling or breaking the rope. He could think of a lot of things that could go wrong. But he stopped himself, refusing to feel scared.

Elsa noticed the fear in Little Rock's eyes. "You'll be okay," she said. "We won't let you fall."

"Oh, I know," Little Rock said, taking a deep breath. "I can do this." He tried to be fearless, just like Anna and Elsa.

Elsa checked to make sure the rope was fastened around Little Rock nice and tight. "Okay," she said. "You ready?"

Little Rock nodded.

Elsa gave everyone at the top the signal and they started to pull. As his body began to rise up along the frozen waterfall, Little Rock waved at Elsa, then closed his eyes. The waterfall was much higher than he thought!

"I guess Oaken was right," said Kristoff as he pulled with all his might. "This is one strong rope!"

"And your life is complete now, just like Oaken promised?" asked Anna jokingly.

"My life is complete," he said. "Don't make me laugh! Now pull!"

The group continued to use all their strength as Little Rock slowly rose to the top of the waterfall.

"I made it!" Little Rock exclaimed as he gripped the ledge with both hands and climbed over. Thrilled to be at the top of the waterfall, he untied the rope. "Thank you, guys! That was kind of fun."

Kristoff was relieved that his plan was working. Now they just needed to help Elsa get to the top. "Okay," he said, digging in the snow. "I'm going to make an anchor by securing this rope and throwing it down to Elsa so she can—"

Anna got Kristoff's attention and pointed behind him. He turned around to see Elsa standing there!

"Okay, then," he said. "Forget the snow anchor . . ."

Elsa smiled sheepishly. "I built steps on the waterfall."

Little Rock looked down and saw a series of sturdy ice steps jutting out of the waterfall. "Your powers are amazing! You can build stairs, shelters, and even sleds!" he exclaimed.

Elsa smiled at the compliment. "I was

going to offer to use my magic earlier, but you were all so excited about Sven's and Kristoff's plans—and Anna really wanted to try waterfall climbing. I didn't want to spoil anybody's fun," she said.

"And it was a great plan," said Anna. "I climbed a frozen waterfall!" She was still pretty proud.

Little Rock cleared his throat and turned to Kristoff and Sven. "It was a great plan," he said. Then he reached into his pouch and pulled out a glowing crystal. "Kristoff and Sven, you get to carry this water crystal because you were so inventive with the waterfall."

Kristoff took the crystal and smiled.

"Thanks, Little Rock. That's really nice of you." He placed the glowing crystal into his pocket and told Little Rock he would keep it safe until the ceremony.

As they began walking, Little Rock continued to thank Kristoff. "I really appreciate you helping me try to earn my crystal and get to the ceremony and . . ." His voice trailed off. He wanted to thank Kristoff for everything, but he didn't know how.

Kristoff stopped him. "You're welcome," he said. "You know I'm always here for you. You're like family to me."

Little Rock looked up at him. "Thanks, Kristoff," he said quietly.

"And besides," added Kristoff with a smile,

"I *have* to help you. I'm basically indebted to you for the rest of my life, remember?"

Little Rock chuckled. "Oh, right," he said. "How could I forget?"

"What are you two talking about?" asked Anna curiously.

"Nothing," Little Rock blurted out.

"Oh, come on," said Anna, nudging him.

"Nothing?" said Kristoff. He turned toward Anna. "Not that long ago, Little Rock saved my life. I might not even be here today if it weren't for this guy."

"Well, I don't know if that's really—" Little Rock said, stumbling over his words.

"Wow," said Anna. "That's a story I want to hear!"

"Me too," said Elsa. "Why don't we already know it?"

"That's exactly what I was thinking," said Anna.

"Yay! Another story!" said Olaf, bursting with enthusiasm. "I just love stories."

"Oh, I don't think you guys really want to hear about that," Little Rock said shyly.

"Of course we do," said Anna. "Come on, Little Rock. Please tell us."

"And besides, it doesn't have anything to do with the Northern Lights," Little Rock said. "All the stories you've told have been great Northern Lights stories, and I don't have one of those."

"It does involve something shooting across

the sky, though." Kristoff chuckled. "Go ahead," he coaxed Little Rock. "I can tell it, but you're the only one who hasn't told a story yet, so it seems to me that you should—"

"Okay, okay, okay," interrupted Little Rock. "I'll tell it. But it really wasn't a big deal. And I'm not the best at telling stories. I'm not as good as you guys are. . . ." He swung his hands around his sides, clapping them together, as if trying to muster the confidence to share the story. Finally, as they continued walking along the trail, Little Rock took a big, deep breath and began to talk.

CHAPTER
16

LITTLE ROCK: Okay, okay. One day—
this was before Kristoff and I were
such good friends. I mean, we were
friends . . . sort of. But not like we
are now. I would say hi to him and
he would say hi back . . . or I would
say "Hey, Kristoff" and he would
say "Hey" and stuff like that. Um . . .

I don't think he knew my name . . .
I'm not sure . . . but I knew his. Well,
everyone knew his name, so that
doesn't really mean much, I guess. I
mean, he's *Kristoff*. Everyone knows
that.

So, anyway . . . I'd been studying
plant identification and learning
about how to tell all the different
types of plants from one another.
We had to be able to identify them,
and to know their troll name and
their common name and their uses,
as well as any potential dangers—
basically everything about them. It
was a lot to remember. I don't know

if you've noticed, but there are thousands of plants around here. Many plants are useful to trolls, but they aren't always the best for humans. Humans have to be extra careful and make sure that plants are safe before they eat them. That's why it's important for trolls and humans to have plant knowledge! At least, that's what Grand Pabbie says.

Anyway, we had to be able to tell the alpine hawkweed from the hawkbit, the moss from the lichen, all the different forget-me-nots— oh, I still forget those. And we had little rhymes to help us remember some of them, like:

"ROCK TRIPE BE TASTY
WHEN CRUNCHY AND DRY
BUT AFTER A RAINFALL
YOU MAY SLIP AND FLY."

Ha. I still remember it. Oh—and . . .

"THREE-LOBED CLOVER IS BEST FOR COLDS
BUT FOUR AND FIVE LOBES
ARE GOOD TO RID MOLDS."

So I was really busy learning about plants and Kristoff was always pretty busy with work, and we didn't have a lot of time together.

But one night, Kristoff had come to the valley. We were celebrating someone's birth night. I think it was Bulda's—yes, of course. It was Bulda's birth night. Every year, Kristoff comes and does something extra special for her on her birth night. Anyway, he made a nice big fire in a fire pit he'd built. We all sat around and had a little party for her. He'd brought her a bouquet of flowers and he had his lute with him. He played a song and sang. It was really great. Bulda loved it!

After he played—actually, she made him play the song like four times—a couple of young trolls brought him a sandwich. Bulda always tried to feed him when he came to visit, and since it was her special night, some of the young trolls did it for her. I think they wanted to impress Kristoff.

So we're all sitting there around the fire and the trolls brought Kristoff his sandwich. I was across from Kristoff and Bulda, on the other side of the fire. Everybody was having a great time, laughing and talking, and I saw Kristoff raise the sandwich up to his mouth to take a bite. I looked at the sandwich and I noticed these leaves sticking out of it—they just happened to catch my eye. Even though I could only see part of them, they looked exactly like the leaves of a Tysbast plant, which is delicious to trolls but highly toxic to humans! Without a second to lose, I leapt across the fire pit and knocked the sandwich right out of his mouth!

It went flying high up in the air and shot across the sky. I hit it so hard, it soared right out of the valley! That's what Kristoff meant before when he said something else went flying across the sky. Get it? Anyway, as I smacked the sandwich out of his mouth, I accidentally knocked him over. So he ended up a little bruised and I think he almost lost a tooth—well, it wiggled a bit.

I got a little bumped up, too. I still have my scar from the fire. Can you see the black mark right here?

But it didn't really hurt very much. Anyway. That's all. That's the end of the story. The end.

CHAPTER 17

Everybody loved hearing Little Rock's story. They were all very impressed with his bravery.

"Look at that," said Anna. "You *are* one fearless troll." She nudged him playfully with her elbow. "And a fine storyteller, by the way," she added.

"Wow," said Olaf. "I hope you're around

if I'm ever about to eat poisonous plants, Little Rock."

"He's the best," said Kristoff.

"It wasn't that big a deal," Little Rock said, shuffling his feet. "And we never found the sandwich, so we don't really know for sure whether it would have actually hurt Kristoff to eat it. The young trolls who made it for him were still learning about plants, so it could've been poisonous, I guess. . . . But he may have been perfectly fine."

"But that's not the point," said Kristoff. "That doesn't matter at all."

Little Rock looked at Kristoff with his face twisted into a confused expression. "What do you mean?" he asked. "Maybe you could have just eaten your sandwich and been fine. Maybe it was just a delicious and perfectly safe sandwich that you would have enjoyed—*and* you wouldn't have had bruises."

Kristoff placed a hand on Little Rock's shoulder, stopping him from walking for a moment as he explained. "You jumped over a fire because you thought I was going to get hurt. You were watching out for me," he said. "You were being a great friend *and* you were being very observant by noticing the plant. Not many people or trolls would have been that courageous."

Little Rock looked up at Kristoff with a shy smile on his face. "Oh, it was nothing," he said, waving a hand through the air.

"It *was* something. Something big," said Kristoff happily. "It was the start of our friendship—and it's a pretty great one."

Anna and Elsa smiled, appreciating Kristoff's sweet words.

"You guys should hug now," said Olaf. "A really big, warm one."

Kristoff hugged Little Rock and then playfully tousled his sprout of hair. "Come on," he said. "Let's pick up the pace and go find Grand Pabbie already."

"Onward!" shouted Little Rock, marching ahead and feeling like the luckiest troll in the world.

As they continued walking up the mountain trail, Little Rock looked at the sky, trying to gauge how much time they had left. It was the final night of autumn. The crystal ceremony would start soon, and Little Rock couldn't help wondering if they would make it. "It's getting late," he murmured.

Elsa, Anna, and Kristoff exchanged a look. They knew exactly what Little Rock was thinking, and they were wondering the very same thing. In fact, they were really starting to worry.

"But we still have time," said Kristoff optimistically.

Little Rock nodded. "A little bit of time to get my tracking crystal to glow *and* find Grand Pabbie." He sighed.

"Don't give up, Little Rock," said Anna.

"You never know—we could turn the next corner and find him."

"I know," said Little Rock. "But you know what? Maybe it doesn't matter. Maybe it's like what Kristoff said about the sandwich . . . maybe it doesn't matter at all."

"No, this is different," said Kristoff. "It matters."

Little Rock stopped walking and turned to face the group. "I need to tell you all something."

"Okay, but don't you think maybe we should keep walking while you tell us?" said Kristoff, feeling anxious.

"No," said Little Rock firmly. "This has been the best adventure I've ever been on, and I've made all of these great new friends. Whether we make it or not, that's the best part. I know that's all that really matters."

The group smiled at Little Rock, touched by his thoughtful words.

"I see what you mean," said Kristoff. "I'm glad you've been having a good time—I know I have. I still am."

The group agreed. The journey had been a great adventure for them all.

But as happy as Kristoff, Anna, and Elsa were to hear Little Rock say that he appreciated the journey, they still wanted him to succeed in his quest. After all his hard work, he deserved the tracking crystal, and to be in the ceremony. They were determined to try their best to help him complete his quest.

"Hey," said Elsa. "Maybe we should pick up the pace." She started to walk faster. "Just for a little bit. Can everyone do that?"

"This trail is pretty straightforward. Let's run!" said Anna. The others joined her.

"Last one to the top is a rotten herring!" said Kristoff, laughing and sprinting ahead of everyone.

"Oh no you don't!" said Anna.

"Okay, but only because I don't want to be a rotten herring," said Little Rock. "I don't know what that is, but it sounds terrible!"

"Wait up! My legs are short! And I don't have any muscles!" said Olaf, running as fast as he could. Sven slowed and let Olaf hop up onto his head. Then he tossed Olaf onto his back and dashed ahead.

"This is the best thing ever!" shouted Olaf, holding Sven's antlers tightly as he bounced up and down.

The group laughed as they chased each other up the mountain trail, running higher and higher. Soon the air filled with mist. As they continued, the mist turned into a fog so dense that they were forced to slow down. The fog became thicker and thicker until it was difficult to see the trail.

"I think we have to take it slow," said Little Rock. "There could be a cliff ahead, for all we know."

"Good idea," said Kristoff. "Take it real slow. One foot in front of the other."

"What a delightful mist," said Olaf. "It makes my snow all tingly."

"I can't believe we're still going up," said Anna, slowly walking alongside Little Rock. "We must be really high."

Little Rock was beginning to feel nervous again. He grabbed Anna's hand and walked with her. Then he began repeating the three rules of tracking like a mantra, focusing on the words rather than his fear: "Be fearless, be observant, be inventive. . . . Be fearless, be observant, be inventive. . . . Be fearless, be observant, be inventive. . . ."

They kept walking up the incline. As they climbed higher, the fog began to dissipate. When they reached the top of the trail, a figure appeared in the mist.

CHAPTER 18

"LOOK!" ANNA SHOUTED.

Kristoff's face lit up as the fog seemed to
magically lift and the figure came into view.
"Grand Pabbie," he said, thrilled to see the
old troll.

"Grand Pabbie!" exclaimed Little Rock,
jumping in the air. He landed on both feet
and ran straight up to a large, moss-covered

boulder on the ground nearby. "We found you!" He threw his arms around the mossy rock and hugged it tight. "I'm so happy!"

Kristoff cleared his throat, trying to get Little Rock's attention. "Um . . . Little Rock?" he said quietly. Then he gestured to the actual Grand Pabbie.

Little Rock stared at Grand Pabbie, a little confused. He looked at the moss-covered rock he was hugging. Then he looked back at Grand Pabbie. Then back at the rock. Finally, it clicked.

"I found him!" he exclaimed, running to Grand Pabbie and giving him a giant hug. "I tracked you, Grand Pabbie."

Grand Pabbie smiled kindly at the little

troll. "Hello, Little Rock," he greeted him.

Little Rock grabbed his crystal pouch and loosened the string. He pulled out his tracking crystal, expecting to see a beautiful glow emanating from it . . . but it was still dull. Little Rock's expression dropped as it registered. The dull crystal meant only one thing: he had *not* earned his tracking crystal. He had failed in his quest.

Everyone gasped, shocked and confused as they took in the sight of the lifeless crystal.

Little Rock looked down at the ground, disappointed. Kristoff moved toward him. "I bet there's something wrong with the crystal," he said, trying to make sense of it.

"Yes, there must be something wrong,"

agreed Anna, trying to reassure Little Rock.

Kristoff inspected the crystal in Little Rock's hand. "It's probably just defective. I'm sure that happens sometimes." He turned to Grand Pabbie. "Right? Can you take a look at it, Grand Pabbie?"

Little Rock held up his hand. "Thanks, guys, but I don't think that's it," he said. "I have something I want to say." Little Rock straightened up as he addressed the group. "I have to tell you all . . . I am not very good at tracking."

Elsa, Anna, and Kristoff began to disagree, but Little Rock stopped them.

"No, no. Really," he continued. "I'm terrible. And you know what? I might never get this tracking crystal to glow." He held up the dull crystal and waved it around as he continued. "The only reason we made it this far is because of you guys. I would have never found Grand Pabbie on my own."

"I don't think that's entirely true . . . ," started Kristoff.

Little Rock shook his head. "It's okay, Kristoff. After our adventures, I've finally seen that I can't track on my own. If anyone here has earned a tracking crystal, it's all of you. I needed you, my friends, to get here. I may not be a great tracker, but I do have great friends."

Suddenly, Little Rock's tracking crystal pulsed with life and started to glow!

"Look!" said Anna, pointing at the shimmering crystal.

Little Rock held it up, perplexed. "Wh-what? H-how?" he stammered.

Grand Pabbie smiled proudly and patted Little Rock on the back. "Very good, Little Rock, very good," said the wise old troll. "Congratulations. You have earned your final level-one crystal: your tracking crystal."

"But I *didn't* earn it—" Little Rock started.

"Remember," said Grand Pabbie. "Crystals shine when a troll gains the skills necessary to be successful. Your tracking crystal is glowing because you did just that. You know you must get a little help from your friends in order to successfully track. I also have to say that you demonstrated very inventive thinking by realizing that."

"I did it?" asked Little Rock in disbelief.

"You did it," said Grand Pabbie.

"I did it!" Little Rock exclaimed, jumping up and down. He rushed over to his friends as they clapped their hands and cheered, congratulating him with kind words and hugs. Sven gave Little Rock a big, slobbery lick across the cheek.

At that moment, other young trolls stepped out of hiding. "Hooray for Little Rock!" they cheered. Little Rock couldn't believe his eyes—it was the other level-one trolls! He greeted them and introduced them to his new friends.

Grand Pabbie gestured toward the sky. The Northern Lights were dancing faintly above them. Turning to Little Rock, he explained, "The cloud cover is not present way up here, so we chose this as the location for the crystal ceremony. We've all been waiting here for you to find us *and* to earn your last crystal. And you have. So now, as autumn prepares to take its rest . . ." Grand Pabbie leaned over to Little Rock and winked as he whispered, "Cutting it a wee bit close with the whole final-night-of-autumn thing, but we're good." He turned back to face everyone. "Let us begin the ceremony."

CHAPTER 19

LITTLE ROCK STOOD WITH THE OTHER young trolls as Grand Pabbie took his place on a nearby boulder. Faint stars twinkled above as the green Northern Lights slowly spread across the sky.

"Now, may I have all the level-one trolls up here, please?" Grand Pabbie said, gesturing to an open area.

The trolls took their places, standing next to one another as Grand Pabbie formally welcomed everyone to the ceremony.

"You have all made long journeys to be here, and that makes tonight very special. Thank you, everyone." He turned to the young trolls. "You may remove your crystals from your pouches."

"Oh," said Little Rock, looking over at Anna and Kristoff. "I need my crystals now."

Anna and Kristoff removed the glowing crystals they'd been carrying and handed them to Little Rock. He turned to Grand Pabbie and the others to explain. "They helped me so much that I thought they deserved to carry crystals, too."

Grand Pabbie smiled. "How very generous of you, Little Rock," he said. "Showing your gratitude in such a personal way was an admirable choice." He motioned for Kristoff and Anna to come closer. "That is a great honor Little Rock bestowed upon you. He worked very hard for those."

"Oh, we know," said Kristoff.

"We are very honored," said Anna. "And honored to be here as well."

As everyone settled in, Grand Pabbie looked up at the sky. The green lights were now joined by hints of pink that were slowly creeping into the pockets of darkness.

Grand Pabbie raised his arms, and the trolls raised their crystals. As the trolls held the glowing rocks in the air, the Northern Lights were reflected in the crystals and seemed to bounce back into the sky, intensifying before their eyes. As the green and pink lights brightened, soft shades of blue appeared.

"These are adequate," said Grand Pabbie. "But I typically prefer brighter lights for ceremonies. The young trolls have worked very hard and they deserve a most memorable night. But we can make it work."

"It's okay with me," said Little Rock, who couldn't stop smiling. "This is already a most memorable night!"

"Grand Pabbie," said Elsa. "Mind if I try something? I may be able to help. . . ."

Grand Pabbie nodded. "Of course, Your

Majesty. Please. We would be honored." As Elsa stepped toward him, he whispered, "I was hoping you might say that." His eyes twinkled like two bright stars as he smiled at her.

Elsa waved her arms, and her magic curled high up into the sky toward the lights. Suddenly, a massive snowflake appeared above. The magnificent sculpture glistened and sparkled as it slowly turned, reflecting the Northern Lights and blasting intense streams of color back into the sky, all around them, and even *on* them! The vibrant colors cast down on everyone, giving them a magical glow and making them look exquisite.

Olaf hopped with excitement as he looked

down at the colors reflected on his body. "I'm a rainbow!" he gasped. "Colorful snow, I love you even more! You're just as happy and amazing as I'd imagined!"

Elsa's and Anna's dresses shimmered with an iridescent radiance. It was as if they were *made* of the Northern Lights!

The dazzling light show left everyone breathless. It was awe-inspiring!

"Well now," said Grand Pabbie, basking in the glow. "That is *so* much better!" He turned to Elsa and bowed his head. "Thank you very much, Your Majesty."

"Anytime," said Elsa, nodding graciously.

Grand Pabbie cleared his throat and began. "We are here because these young trolls have earned their level-one crystals. This is a special achievement they have all worked very hard to attain. We honor them by gathering here tonight under these extraordinary Northern Lights."

Grand Pabbie went on to explain the importance of the crystals and how they represented a troll's connection to nature. "For trolls, this is the beginning of a lifelong responsibility to nurture both the earth and sky," Grand Pabbie said. "We trolls must do our part to make the crystals glow, and in turn, the crystals help keep the Northern Lights alive."

He and the trolls joined together as they said:

"WE GUARDIANS OF EARTH DO KNOW
AUTUMN LIGHTS AND CRYSTALS GLOW
SO OUR BOND MAY DEEPEN AND GROW."

Anna leaned over to Elsa. "I think I get it now," she whispered. "Maybe? A little? Sort of?"

Elsa smiled at her sister. They were both just happy to be there.

As the ceremony continued, the trolls were invited to talk about one of their crystal-earning experiences. Of course, Little Rock chose to tell about his tracking crystal. Kristoff, Anna, Elsa, Olaf, and Sven watched proudly as Little Rock briefly described the journey they had gone on together.

"And now these young trolls will have

memories of their own to share," Grand Pabbie said. "As their crystals and bonds have strengthened, we will all enjoy the wondrous view that such strength and honor can offer." Then he turned to the trolls. "Please hold your crystals up once again."

This time, when they raised their crystals, the Northern Lights were reflected in them and bounced back into the sky. The lights became brighter still, dancing across the night in a bursting display. With Elsa's snowflake still slowly spinning above, it was the most incredible Northern Lights display anyone had ever seen!

Up on top of the mountain peak, surrounded by so many loved ones, Little

Rock felt proud and grateful. As they all enjoyed the Northern Lights together, he smiled. He looked at his friends and took a moment to etch the image into his memory, knowing that now he had his very own Northern Lights story to share.

Far away, in Troll Valley, the intense colors quickly caught Bulda's eye. "Look!" she shouted. "Everybody, look up!"

All the trolls gazed at the sky. They knew what the bright lights meant: Little Rock had succeeded in his quest and all was as it should be. Thanks to the success of the level-one trolls, the Northern Lights were shining and thriving, providing everyone below with magical memories.

CHAPTER 20

ARENDELLE WAS BUZZING WITH activity as the tired travelers entered through the city gates.

"Good day!" sang friendly voices.

Anna and Elsa smiled and returned the cheerful greetings.

It had been an incredible journey, full of fun, friendship, and adventure. But as much as they'd enjoyed their trip, they felt happy to be home again.

Once they reached the courtyard, Anna asked her friends if they had any last thoughts to write in the adventure journal. To her surprise, each of them had something they wanted to add. Even Sven left his mark as he dripped a little slobber on the book while giving it a big lick.

Anna thanked them for contributing. "This will be such a special addition to our library," she said. "Just think: for years to come, people can read all about our Northern Lights adventure."

"It was a really great idea, Anna," said Elsa. "People can learn all about the trolls' crystal ceremony and how to earn a tracking crystal."

"And how to be a good friend," added Olaf. "That's the best part!"

"You did write about us climbing the frozen waterfall, right? That's got to be a great read," Kristoff said.

"Of course!" exclaimed Anna. "You think I'd leave that out?" She chuckled. "That reminds me . . . when are we doing that again?"

"You know me," replied Kristoff. "I'm always up for ice climbing."

"After a nice bath and a good night's sleep, I'll be ready and waiting," said Anna. "With my metal spikes strapped on and an ax in hand."

"You're such a mountain woman," Kristoff teased.

Everyone knew it was time to say goodbye and get some rest. They thanked Kristoff for taking them on the journey.

"Thank *you* all," he said. "It was the best kind of adventure because—"

"It was full of surprises," said Anna and Elsa. "We know, we know."

"Nope," Kristoff said, shaking his head. "Because it was with my best friends."

"Awww," Anna and Elsa said, smiling at him.

"You should hug now," said Olaf. "We should all hug. Warm group hug! Yay!"

They shared the warmest group hug

Arendelle had ever seen, and then they parted ways.

Gerda and Kai smiled as they welcomed Elsa and Anna home.

"You look like you've been on a quite a journey," said Kai.

"Oh, we certainly have," Elsa replied.

"It was amazing!" Anna added. "But as fun as it was, I'm looking forward to curling up in my nice warm bed."

"And actually sleeping at night again," Elsa laughed.

"How about some tea before you turn in?"

Gerda asked. The girls nodded and Gerda turned to walk toward the kitchen. Then she paused and looked back at them. "Or maybe some hot cocoa instead?"

"Yes!" the girls exclaimed.

"That sounds wonderful," said Anna.

"It's waiting for you by the fire," said Kai with a smile.

The sisters thanked them and rushed into the study. They sat down and reminisced about the trip. They both agreed: they had never seen the Northern Lights look so bright.

"Did you wish on them?" asked Anna with a knowing smile.

Elsa nodded. "Of course. Did you?"

Anna nodded.

"I wished for more adventures with my sister," they said together.

The sisters laughed and clinked their mugs of hot cocoa, enjoying each other's company and the new memories they'd made.